We Go On

Anthology for Veterans Charities

We Go On © Dec 2014, Kiki Howell, Editor

Special Thanks

I would like to give a special, from the bottom of my heart, thank you to my family for donating money to make this dream of editing an anthology for veterans' charities a reality. I absolutely could not have done it without you.

I'd also like to thank all of the authors who dedicated their time and talent.

As well, I'd like to give a huge amount of thanks to family and friends, you know who you are, who listened to me stress throughout this process. I owe you for keeping me sane and focused by listening and loving me. I treasure your words of advice. And, to one special friend who not only listened, or maybe I should say read all my frantic messages, but also gave me tons of help with her publishing expertise, my unending thanks. You know who you are lady, and I'm blessed to have you in my life.

4

Table of Contents

Still, *We Go On*

Honor Bound even on peaceful soil, year after year
Excellence In All We Do manifests in turmoil
What's done for *Duty* and *Respect* my mind can't reconcile
Loyalty falls short when a friend born of war dies again in my dream

But, *We Go On*

This We'll Defend echoes still as we battle only for normalcy
"If a man does his best, what else is there?" I hear Patton say
Yet, *Personal Courage* no longer prevails as triggers rattle me
So, *No Mission Too Difficult*, we find ways to numb

Steadfast, *We Go On…*

Dedicated to combat veterans and PTSD sufferers,
wherever they may be...thank you for your service...

An Enemy That Haunts My Mind
by Alan W. Jankowski

In the middle of the night I lie in bed,
Fighting an enemy that's in my head.
An enemy that's always there,
An enemy that won't play fair.
An enemy that haunts my mind,
An enemy that is not kind.
The price paid for doing good,
Of doing like I'm told I should.
Serving my country in time of war,
Who could ever ask for more?
And now even in my deepest dreams,
All I hear is the sound of screams.
Why was I the one to survive?
Why was I the one left alive?
I ask myself every night,
As I relive every fight.
God, please call me home,
Don't leave me here all alone.
For when I thought the fight was won,
I'm finding the battle's just begun.
A soldier who was trained to kill,
Finds a battle that's harder still.
Fighting an enemy I cannot see,
And finding out the enemy is me.
An enemy that haunts my mind,
An enemy that is not kind.

About the Author:

Alan W. Jankowski is the award winning author of well over one hundred short stories, plays and poems. His stories have been published online, and in various journals including Oysters & Chocolate, Muscadine Lines: A Southern Journal, eFiction Magazine, Zouch, The Rusty Nail, and a few others he can't remember at the moment. His poetry has more recently become popular, and his 9/11 Tribute poem was used extensively in ceremonies starting with the tenth anniversary of this tragic event.

When he is not writing, which is not often, his hobbies include music and camera collecting. He currently resides in New Jersey. He always appreciates feedback of any kind on his work, and can be reached by e-mail at: Exakta66@gmail.com

Wailing Wall
by Judith Turner-Yamamoto

"Meet me at the apex, that's where he is, the apex,"
Charlie Markham's voice, that of a man who had spent a
lifetime working with airplanes and loud machinery,
boomed in Vivian's ear. "How's ten o'clock do you?"

"Fine," Vivian said, holding the phone away from her
ear, awaiting his confirmation.

"Don't forget your yellow scarf."

"No, no, I won't."

"That a girl."

He was gone, too busy or too distracted for hellos or
good-byes.

Aimless, Vivian paused before the mirror, adjusting
again the yellow silk scarf she'd bought just for this
occasion. The yellow scarves had been Charlie's idea.

"How will we know each other? The Mall will be
mobbed on Veteran's day," she'd asked when they'd first
planned their meeting months ago.

"Yellow scarves," he'd answered right away, as
though he had carried the picture of the two of them
standing out in the crowd in this same way for a long
time.

Reminded of the welcoming yellow ribbons that had
dressed up car antennas and rung trees in her small
Iowa town during Desert Storm, she had agreed.

Her motel room window looked out on the parking lot
and a four-lane highway just beyond. It was, she
imagined, the kind of view people wanted when they
were committing immoral acts. Nonjudgmental, neutral,
like the blank stare of a stranger, the abundant blacktop
offered nothing to remind one of their place in a
particular community. She could be anywhere, back in
Iowa even. But, if she stood to one side of the plate
glass, if she angled her head just so, she could see the
Iwo Jima Memorial, the monument her motel had been
named for. There, immortalized in bronze, five soldiers
struggled to plant an American flag in the loose volcanic

11

soil of a distant Japanese island. Their colossal size and effort bore witness to the gravity of their cause. Their solidarity made her think of her fiancé, Vinny, with George and Charlie, three crewmen on a cargo plane flying low over the jungles of Vietnam.

She'd spent all yesterday visiting monuments to heroes big and small, preparing herself for today. Starting in Arlington National Cemetery at the graves of the Union soldiers buried in General Lee's rose garden, she then worked her way down through the Cemetery to the Virginia banks of the Potomac River before moving onto Roosevelt Island, the Jefferson Memorial, and the Washington Monument. Finally, fingers numb from the cold, cheeks stinging from the ceaseless east wind with its curious marine smell, she stumbled toward the Lincoln Memorial in the premature November night.

Pausing to rest her aching, lower back, she chose a bench facing the Vietnam Veterans Memorial. She felt the certain pull of the V-shaped, black granite walls reaching out of the earth to the Washington Monument and the Lincoln Memorial, toward the founding and preservation of the nation, and to her. Assured of its presence, she had gone on, up the marble steps, into the light of the Lincoln Memorial. For the first time in forty-five years she walked where Vinny's name had been etched. All this time, thinking she was the only one who cared. Now there was Charlie Markham.

Vivian's trip to Washington had been seven years in the planning. Seeing Vinny's name on a traveling version of the memorial made her realize that years of therapy, a string of failed relationships, and the years of living she'd done since his death hadn't begun to touch the depth of her grief.

Carrying ammunition, downed by a barrage of gunfire in the dense jungle, Vinny's plane had gone up in gluttonous flames. There was no body, no flag-draped coffin, no gravesite, and thus no possibility for what the grieving experts described as closure until this monument called the Wall. Still, like an astrologer

12

waiting for the planets to align, she had deferred coming, waiting for a coalescence of significant events.

She watched the passage of his fortieth birthday, then hers, and then the fortieth anniversary of his death. She held out for the moment when enough things coming together at once would ease her beyond the ache that had become as involuntary as breathing.

"You're married to your pain, how could you possibly become involved with anyone else?" her therapist had told her. The carefully chosen words had resonated but changed nothing.

Submitting her name and Vinny's to the database for the Vietnam Veterans Memorial, she'd heard from Charlie, Vinny's navigator.

Meet me at the Wall? Veteran's Day. He'd written, giving her a Washington address and phone number. Tearing through Vinny's old letters, she'd found the staccato notes Charlie had scribbled in the margins on the backs of envelopes.

This guy's nuts, you want him? Wise up, take me.

Today was Veterans Day, November 11, the date she and Vinny had set for their wedding. His name had been on the Wall for more years than she wanted to count. Vinny's best friend was alive and waiting to meet her. She pulled the drapes on her qualified view, gathered her bag, the keys to her rental car, and headed downtown.

All of Constitutional Gardens appeared a swarm of camouflage green, but Charlie Markham wasn't hard to find. He stood at the juncture of the east and west walls, a big man, nearly seventy, with faded fatigues layered under a down jacket, an Air Force cap topping a close clipped head of gray hair, and a yellow pilled muffler around his neck. He'd suggested yellow scarves as a matter of convenience then. Clasping her scarf to her throat, she worked her way past her disappointment, through the crowd of Vietnam vets and their families.

Somehow she had expected him to look like the snapshot Vinny had once sent her of the two of them,

13

shirtless, dog tags shining carelessly in the foreign sun. What of the lines around her own eyes, the veil of white over her black hair? Endless youth was for Vinny and for the others who had died young.

Charlie waved one end of his scarf in the air. "Viv," he called, using Vinny's name for her.

When she reached him, he took her arm, turned her toward the wall.

"Here he is, row fifteen, sixth from the left. There's George, right below him. I always liked it, the two of them ending up together. They say they put them in the order they died. How do they know that? People were dying all over the place. Nobody had a stopwatch did they, going around... Oh God, I'm sorry. I'm talking like some tour guide and here you are..."

He handed her a thick, graphite pencil and a black-bordered piece of white paper. "I figured you'd want a rubbing. The supplies were going fast today." He jammed his empty hands in his pockets, then gestured awkwardly at the Wall. "I'll leave you alone."

Vinny's name was in reach. Her face, the face of an old woman, reflected over his name. More than she'd hoped for, she stepped close, ran her fingers across the letters and felt the great hardness of the polished granite. Positioning her paper, she stroked the pencil across his name, watching him emerge like an apparition from the velvet of the graphite. This she could take away. This was all. She stared at the rubbing, before she placed it with care in her bag.

"Let's walk the wall," Charlie said beside her, his hand on her upper arm, lending the support she hadn't realized she'd needed. They began where the west wall emerged from the ground. She counted five names, then more. As the wall rose, the names increased, until it became impossible to grasp the numbers.

Two small boys hung from the Wall, hands inching along its growing height. A uniformed park ranger strode toward them, but Charlie reached them first, looping a long arm around each one.

14

"Not here, boys," he said as he sat them down gently, knelt in front of them, tousling their hair. "Go on, find your parents."

Charlie's manner, the sight of his big hand on the boys' heads brought Vivian to sudden tears. She turned away, focusing instead on the offerings left along the narrow trench at the base of the Wall. The rubbing of a name done on a napkin lay closest. '*J. Hall was here'* scribbled on a crumpled grocery receipt. A lone cigarette housed in a plastic baggy. A plastic funeral wreath teetered on thin metal legs. Three names underlined, like things to remember to do, were written on a page torn from a "Your American Family Agent" note pad.

Charlie stopped to look at a silver ID bracelet.

"Twice a day they pick this stuff up and it just keeps coming. It's a never ending wake, a wailing wall," he explained.

Vivian stepped around a woman her mother's age. One hand held a red rose pressed against the wall, while the other shielded her eyes from the sight. The gleaming, black stone cradled the names, the woman, the sky, the bare trees, the crowd of strangers, her and Charlie in its reflection.

"God is ten thousand things," Charlie said, as though he knew what she felt. "The Buddhists say that. I always think of it when I come here."

"What happened, Charlie? With Vinny, I mean," she said, the words tearing at her throat.

"It's never clean, the explanation, they make sure of that. I tried for years, but they gave me all kinds of answers. Snipers. Engine failure. Pilot error. That last one got me. I quit asking after they hit me with that."

He stopped, lit a cigarette, and dropped the snuffed match in the shirt pocket of his fatigues.

"I wasn't on that run. I guess you've figured that out. They had sent me to another base supporting bombing raids to replace a navigator who'd gone home," he offered and then inhaled deeply, the smoke rolling into the cold air, a sudden fog. "Ten months the three of us ran that trash hauler in and out of the jungle, carrying supplies. Sometimes the screaming wounded and the body bags we picked up for the hospitals. It was an easy run they were doing to a base we'd serviced a million times. What do you think? They got lazy, depended on me too much? Why wasn't I with them?" he spoke in a low voice meant for himself. "I've never stopped asking myself those questions."

She laced her fingers around the bulky sleeve of his jacket, gave his arm the best squeeze she could manage. "You didn't write your orders, you didn't desert them, if that's what you've let yourself believe."

They found themselves back by Vinny and George's names. Charlie's hand covered hers. The warmth of his thick fingers traveled through her gloves.

"I kept thinking there's a reason, something special I'm supposed to do. So I became an air traffic controller. I kept planes from crashing into one another. That's the best I've been able to come up with. What about you?"

"Me?"

"You're here, aren't you?"

She ran her hand over Vinny's inscription, each letter concisely rounded, definite. How could she tell Charlie she meant to finally give Vinny up, to leave the part of him here with his name that had lived in her so long, when she wasn't sure she wanted to let him go? She turned aside, gave Charlie a vague shrug she hoped would end his questions.

"I always meant to come, but I put it off," she offered.

Charlie shrugged back. "Okay, you don't have to talk about it."

He took a deck of cards and a yellowed bit of newspaper from his jacket pocket. He nodded in Vinny's direction.

"Crazy Eights, we used to play that between flights to keep from going crazy. You bring anything for him?"

Vivian opened her bag and took out a small black leather box.

"Engagement ring?" Charlie asked.

16

Vivian nodded, the knuckles of the hand holding the box showing white. He'd been dead five years before she could bring herself to move the ring to her right hand. Another five passed before she stopped wearing it altogether, placing it in the drawer of her jewelry chest where she kept her best things. Just four years ago, she had consigned the ring to her bank safe deposit box along with the bulk of his letters, her grandmother's pearls, her will, and her modest investments in stocks and bonds.

"He had it engraved with a W. That's two V's really, like us." She bit the inside of her bottom lip, checking the urge to tell him unrevealed things.

Charlie eased the box from her hand, undid the clasp. "Go on, put it on, Viv."

Fingers shaking, Vivian slipped the diamond on, watched the small stone catch the light. "It's a girl's ring, meant for young hands."

"It's beautiful," Charlie said, closing her fingers around the open box.

Vivian knelt down, placing the ring box beside Charlie's things. *Talk, please talk,* she thought. *Talk,* because I can't.

Charlie helped her to her feet, his hands staying on her elbow, under her forearm. He pointed to the scrap of newsprint.

"His death notice. I left the other half in Nepal. I found this little shrine to a Monkey God, the face nearly worn off from the constant touching. I buried half the notice under some broken stones. Half was all I could give up," he said in a low voice.

Vivian took a bottle of champagne and a corkscrew from her bag.

"This was for his homecoming," she explained.

She turned the cork inside her coat, muffling the pop she'd always imagined being as loud as an Independence Day firecracker. She handed Charlie two, wrapped, plastic cups from her motel room.

She asked, "Would you do the honors?"

17

She lifted the insubstantial cup to her lips, the smell of new plastic confusing the sparkling bouquet of the drink. Silent, they toasted Vinny, George, and each other. Charlie swirled the last of his champagne, and then threw it back in one gulp like bitter medicine. Vivian did the same.

She let out a long sigh, "When I die, I want all our letters left at the wall. You're in those letters too, you know? Do you remember the notes you would scratch on the envelopes, in the margins? I brought one to show you."

Charlie ran his fingers over his handwriting, the ink smeared and faded. "God, I can remember this night. It was pouring rain. I can smell it, the soil trying to keep up, absorbing all that rain. You know that smell?"

Vivian shook her head.

"Death does that, the prospect of it, it wakes you up to life. We were all like that. I don't think we were ever more alive." He grabbed her hand. "Come on, I want to show you something."

He led her to a Greek temple set in a copse of trees beyond the Lincoln Memorial. Vivian stepped inside the column-enclosed circumference, a space no larger than her own living room, pocked and blackened by commuter exhaust.

"What is this place?" she inquired.

"D.C. War Memorial. Honors the city's dead from World War I. Their names are inscribed around the base. Nobody comes here to mourn anymore," Charlie dug his toe against a loose chunk of marble. "The ones who do come, they don't have the pain. People get married here. You see them every weekend in the spring and summer. The hats. The bright dresses. The musicians. All of them smiling, dancing."

He paused a moment, steadying, she knew, the unexpected wobble in his voice, then he continued, "You think the Wall will ever be like that, a place where you can dance?"

She put her arms around him, sliding her hands beneath his jacket to where his fatigues pulled tight across his shoulders. "Charlie? I know why I didn't come. I was afraid to let go of him, afraid he was all there was."

"There's a dance tonight, Delta to the DMZ. Wanna go?"

"Sure," she said. "But why wait?"

Vivian took off her scarf, then Charlie's. Knotting them together, she tied the unlikely ribbon around one of the columns. She pulled him to the center of the temple, planted his arm around her waist and settled her hand on his shoulder.

"The skies open up and put people in our path to help us. Do you believe that, Charlie?"

Together, they began to move in a slow syncopated rhythm.

The End

About the Author:

Judith Turner-Yamamoto's awards include residency fellowships from the Virginia Center for the Creative Arts and Fundacíon Valparaiso, Manchester Fiction Prize Short List, Story Quarterly Scholar, Sewanee Writers' Conference; the Thomas Wolfe Fiction Prize, the Virginia Governor's Screenwriting Award, two Individual Artist Fellowships from the Virginia Commission on the Arts, and a Moving Words Poetry Prize from Arlington County, Virginia Arts Council. She has been a finalist for numerous additional awards, including the Sundance Institute Screenwriters Workshop.

Her stories and poems have appeared in magazines and journals, including *The Mississippi Review, The American Literary Review, Verdad, The Village Rambler, Parting Gifts, Potomac Review, Dart,* and *Snake Nation*

Review. Anthologies featuring her work include *Gravity Dancers*, Paycock Press, 2009, *Double Lives*, 2009, and *Best New Poets 2005.* She has taught fiction at the Writers' Center at the Chautauqua Institution, the Danville Writer's Conference, and at the Writers' Center in Bethesda, Maryland.

An art historian, she is a critic and features writing covering the arts, design, and travel for *Travel & Leisure, Elle, USAir, Art & Antiques*, *Interiors,* and *The Boston Globe Magazine*, among others. She is an on-air interviewer for *Around Cincinnati*, a weekly arts talk show on NPR station WVXU.

I would like to dedicate this poem to the Marks, big and little (my father and brother), Honorable Marines who inspire me always.

A Soldier's Dream
by Steve Morse

One night
I had a dream,
a glorious dream.

I was a young man,
Bright-eyed,
my face smooth,
unblemished.

I stood tall
And proud.
My close cropped hair as
impeccable
as my new uniform,
sharp.
I was a soldier.

The dream shifted
as dreams do.

I walked through a village
in a mountainous
desert land.
My hair had grown
ragged,
stubble conquered my
smooth face,
and
lines sought refuge
at the corners of my
desert faded
eyes.

The villagers saw me
in my
mottled brown
uniform,
matching the desert land.
They were polite
and spoke to me in their
rapid, throaty language
smiling
but
not
their
eyes.

Rancor arose in
the village
marketplace.
We ran toward it,
my fellow soldiers and I,
to investigate.

Around a corner
a small
homemade
device,
unseen.
The world flashed white.

The dream shifted
as dreams do.
I lay in a room of sterile light
surrounded,
pinned down
by hostile faces
I recognized.
They were polite
And smiled
but not

their
eyes.

The dream shifted
as dreams do.

I sat
huddled in the corner
of my small
lightless room.
Sweat drenched,
trembling
as the thunder
roared,
clutching my knife.
Screaming when
the world flashed white.

Once more,
the dream shifted,
as dreams do.

The man stood
dapper in his
three-piece suit
"Thank you for your service
to our country,"
he said,
"but I'm afraid we cannot
hire you.
It's the economy,"
he explained.
I could feel the revulsion
as he shook
my three-fingered
hand
and dodged
my surviving eye.
He was polite

and smiled
A gleaming,
expensive
smile,
but not his
eyes.

One night I had a dream
at least,
I pray,
it was only a dream.

About the Author:

Steve Morse is a son to a career Marine. He lived his
early life in Camp Lejune, NC and Camp Pendelton. He
has a Bachelor of English from Humboldt State
University, and currently resides in Portland, Oregon.

For all the military men in my life—family and Veterans. Thank you.

No Man Left Behind
by Terry Rozum

The sign read **Stand Down!** The crudely hand-lettered poster hung by the back door of the rec center at just the right height to read, if you were a giraffe. A Christmas wreath hung just below it, as if an afterthought of the holiday fast approaching. *Stand Down!* —an event sponsored through the Veterans Administration for homeless veterans— is traditionally held during November across the U.S. However, because of a scheduling error in Mobile, Alabama, Uncle Sam was now Uncle Santa holding the event as a community Christmas activity.

Vehicles were parked askew in the makeshift parking lot, or soccer field as it would have been known on any other day. On this blustery December day, men and women in uniform filed quietly into the building like troops on a secret mission. Mobile had never been known for its cold, winter weather, but today stood the exception. A chill was in the air. Clouds hung low, dark, and grey. Much like my spirits.

Arriving early, as usual, I watched as volunteers arrived alone. Some old, some young. Male and female. Some fit, some not so. Their uniforms varied, belonging to service groups representing the VFW, American Legion, DAV, and the Vietnam Veterans Association. Some wore embroidered baseball style caps proudly identifying their service era. Vietnam Veteran. Korean Veteran. World War II Veteran. All had ribbons and medals attached to the vests they wore identifying the veterans' service organization they volunteered with. Older participants still wore the crew-cut hairstyle of their military days. Younger ones had long, unkempt hairstyles and facial hair, a definite nose-thumb in the face of military spit and polish. Most of the volunteers

25

arrived as sole occupants of their well-kept, late model pick-up trucks. Some carried Starbucks cups or insulated mugs of coffee with them. All looked solemn, serious.

I didn't want to be here. I had done everything I could to avoid this situation. Yet, being the most recent hire at the Mobile VA clinic, I'd been forced into service. I hated feeling trapped almost as much as I hated feeling helpless. Waiting in my car looking for a familiar face to walk in with me and finding none, I walked quietly into the building alone. Head down, eyes focused on the ground.

My thoughts were on the Christmas Eve gathering I was to attend at my family's homestead later in the evening. It wasn't often that the entire clan was able, or willing for that matter, to gather. Coming from a family filled with career military members made it difficult to pull everyone together. Someone was always stationed in a different part of the world or just about to be deployed. Tonight would be the first gathering since my job change. I dreaded the ribbing I knew I would receive about my career choice, having chosen social service instead of military service as my contribution to society. Spending the evening in the company of family veterans was enough to strike fear into the heart of this social worker, although I looked forward to seeing family members I hadn't seen in a while.

I knew the spread on the kitchen table would be exceptional, and the house would be decorated with Christmas heirlooms collected from all over the world. I couldn't wait to smell the tobacco scent from my dad's pipe as he told the Christmas story to the youngsters, and to see which Christmas sweater my mom would be wearing this year. I loved seeing my nieces in their hand-embroidered outfits and hearing my nephews singing their potty-mouth versions of Christmas carols. I cherished the knowledge that my family loved me even when they teased me about being a tree-hugging soul.

My focus now was to spend the day with homeless veterans and then escape to my family celebration.

Inside the rec center, we sat on cold, aluminum, folding chairs at long, narrow tables. The chairs were bent and chipped, mismatched. Every piece of the furniture had seen better days. My holiday sweater kept catching on the ragged edge of the table where it had been chipped and torn from being stacked together with hundreds of other tables in the center. The gray, damp, cinder block building was anything but cheerful, so plates of holiday cookies had been set out on each of the tables. A touch of Christmas spirit served as an invitation to visit that station.

At my table we were to register vets as they entered the rec hall, but there were no pens. Plenty of forms. No pens. Other tables were set up with posters and handouts about local community services for the vets to read. A barber, in his crisp, white barber's apron, stood ready to cut hair. A nurse, wearing medical scrubs, checked her supplies and prepared to do HIV/AIDS testing should anyone ask. A perky, state job counselor sat patiently waiting to dispense advice on where and how to find employment in the area. A doctor, presumably a resident from the local medical school, was available to perform mini-physical exams.

With visions of community service hours dancing in their heads, a junior high school choir stood clustered in the corner, warming up to sing Christmas carols. Their director raised his hands, nodded his head in a down beat, and the choir belted out a hearty version of *God Rest Ye Merry Gentlemen*. As they continued preparations, volunteers turned and grinned as they observed the cherub faces. They finished their first selection and began to sing *I'll Be Home for Christmas*. Perhaps reconsidering it, given the event, the director called a quick halt with a throat slash gesture. The voices choked to a halt as he quickly directed them to another selection.

The gymnasium bleachers had been turned into a makeshift thrift clothing store for this day, with neatly stacked-by-size rows of tee shirts, underwear, socks, sweaters, desert fatigues, and shoes. Toiletry items had been placed in Christmas bags to look like gifts.

In the kitchen area, the scent of bacon filled the air as volunteers cooked breakfast to serve to those who arrived in time. The smell and sound of fresh brewed coffee called to us caffeine junkies.

"Ma'am, could you tell me where to sign up for services?" a man asked, shyly.

His face was almost completely hidden by his thick, unkempt beard. Only his eyes peeked out from under the hair and knit cap. He had kind eyes. His clothes were ragged, but adequate. Soiled, but not dirty.

"Hartshorn, 5678," he stated his last name along with the last four digits of his social security number just to punctuate his request, verifying that he was service connected.

I hurriedly assisted him in signing in, having scrounged a pen from my purse. He finished the short form, and I smiled as I made contact with his ocean blue eyes. I pointed him toward the kitchen so he could get breakfast before they stopped serving. Then I watched as he walked slowly toward the dining area, carrying his backpack over his shoulder and his blanket roll under his arm. His untied shoes softly drug along the gym floor with each step. Without looking at the paperwork he had just completed, I guessed his age to be somewhere in his forties, maybe fifties. I mused at what events must have occurred to this man to cause him to be at this time and place in his life.

Homeless men and women arrived in droves. The rec center was located close enough to the downtown business district that the Government Street Presbyterian Church had volunteered to transport them to the event as they gathered at the church's steps. The vets all looked lost and lonely. They filed in quietly, almost robotically. No one spoke unless spoken to. No one bantered or laughed with anyone, heads down, looking at the floor as they walked or as they answered questions.

Helping them wasn't hard, but it didn't feel like enough. Giving them basic necessities seemed so inadequate. Speaking to them as if they were real people seemed respectful but not their everyday experience. Telling them to have a good day or a happy holiday didn't feel appropriate but was the expected spirit of the day. They appeared appreciative of the food, clothing and personal items offered to them as they filled their rucksacks with items that most Americans take for granted. Most of them took blankets, sweaters, and sleeping bags after they had discarded the filthy, tattered ones they had brought or worn when they'd entered.

"Can you spare a bus pass or two?" was asked in the same way they would have panhandled quarters in Bienville Square.

Hours passed by quickly. Morning turned into late afternoon as we handed out information and registered hundreds of homeless vets for clinic services. Although different and distinct from each other, they blended together as they filed past the tables.

"Hey, remember me?" the newly shorn, clean shaven, smiling man with kind eyes suddenly asked me.

"No, sorry, don't believe I do. Have we met? A lot of guys passed this way today… I don't think I can remember them all," I said, smiling back at him.

"Hartshorn, 5678." He chuckled.

What a difference a few hours had made in this veteran. The man I had thought was approaching middle age now appeared to be about thirty-five, handsome, and happy.

"So, you know my name. What's yours? Or aren't we allowed to know that?" he asked.

Quizzing me seemed to amuse and please him.

"I'm Ms. Phillips," I said, showing him my badge as if to verify my identity. I'd not given my first name to preserve a sense of professional distance.

29

"Pleased to meet you, ma'am," he answered, not having lost that respectful and expected tone used by soldiers in the ranks. "Merry Christmas and thank you for all your help," he added as he walked toward the exit, head held up this time.

The day closed with the volunteers stacking the ragged tables back together again and putting the chairs on the dolly to be rolled into the storage area. The clothing had all been given out. The coffee and cookies had been consumed. We applauded the choir as they sang their closing number, *Grandma Got Run Over by a Reindeer*. Our mission completed, the volunteers began to file out to the parking lot that was now covered with, oddly enough, a light dusting of snow. In the dusk of the day, the soccer field looked magical as the snow glittered and sparkled, illuminated by the lone working street lamp's bluish light.

Driving out of the parking lot, hastily trying to get to my family gathering, I spotted him, Hartshorn 5678, at the city bus stop, sitting on the brick divider wall near the street. He smiled and waved as he watched me drive out and turn toward the western suburbs. I stared into the rear view mirror at his shrinking figure. Reflecting on the day, I could still envision the vets' unshaven and haggard faces. It's hard to forget the face of someone you fear that you could be one day. How did the men and women I met today get here? What choices had they made? What choices hadn't they made? Where were their friends and family members when they needed them? How could this happen in a place with so much abundance? How could this be the fate of men who had once been buff, clean-shaven, military heroes protecting the rights of all the citizens of this nation? Without a second thought, I made a quick U-turn and headed back to the bus stop.

"Hey, Hartshorn, what are you doing for Christmas Eve?" I asked as I rolled down the window, driving up close to the curb.

"Ahh, let me check my calendar." He laughed out loud. "What did ya have in mind?"

"How would you like to spend the evening with a group of military retirees, active duty nerds and geeks, and one idealistic social worker out to save the world one veteran at a time?" I asked with a laugh.

Seemed only appropriate that a military brat should bring home one of her own for a holiday meal. After all, the military claims to be the world's biggest family. Homeless in the world's wealthiest nation? Not as long as there is a military family like mine—at least I hoped they would see it that way.

"By the way, my name's Homer. You gotta first name?" Hartshorn asked as he threw his gear into the back seat.

"Destiny." I smiled, the irony in both our names not escaping me.

The End

About the Author:

Terry Rozum is a Social Worker in Mobile, Alabama. She is a native Alabamian having grown up in Fairhope and attended both Auburn University and the University of Alabama. Terry is passionate about cats, writing, and social work—pretty much in that order. She writes for and is on the editorial staff for the Inspire! newsletter for the Gulf Coast VA and her fiction has been published in several local anthologies.

Waging Peace
by Kelly Talbot

I put my guns down today.
My brother came to kill me
with daggers and dreams. The wind
spoke of rain, and I listened
and was cold. Each drop whispered
of clouded gray skies. They plunged
from heaven on high to come
down and sweetly caress my
upturned face, and they told a
tale of ponderous dark rumblings
that could be felt but not touched.
The hour grew later, the sky
turned darker, the wind howled, and
the water froze, becoming
tiny daggers piercing my
flesh, and I trembled, looking
into the raging heart of
blackness. Riding through the sky
on lightning and thunder in
the midst of his fury, my
brother flew down to kill me
with daggers bristling, and I,
I smiled and laid down my guns.

First published in the magazine Aries *in 2008.*

About the Author:

Kelly Talbot has edited books, digital content, blogs, and web sites for twenty years, previously as an in-house editor for John Wiley and Sons, Macmillan Publishing, and Pearson Education, and now as the head of Kelly Talbot Editing Services. His writing appears in dozens of magazines and anthologies. He divides his time between Indianapolis, Indiana, and Timisoara, Romania. Kelly has the utmost respect for the courage and dedication of the men and women who serve in all branches of the military.

I would like to dedicate this story to my father, Bert Hansen, and all other servicemen and women. Your efforts and sacrifices are greatly appreciated.

Just a Humble Hero
by John Hansen

Jim shuffled restlessly on the slatted bench, an oversized army trench coat his only protection against the chill in the air. Sitting up, he pulled a metal canteen from his coat, unscrewed the cap, and took a swig. When the last mouthful of liquid slid down his throat, he shook the canteen as though hoping it had been magically refilled, but only a few drops flicked out.

Most of the park's residents drank cheap wine, but not Jim. Whisky warmed your body and helped keep the cold at bay. Besides, he had his pride. Nobody could call Jim a wino, a hobo maybe, but never a wino.

Yes, he still had his pride, and his health. For that he was thankful. Everything else was gone. Jim was only fifty-six years old, though he looked ten years older. He scratched the greying stubble on his chin and tried to contemplate his life.

On leaving school he joined an engineering firm as an assistant draftsman, but his career was cut short in 1966 when he was conscripted for National Service. Along with a number of his friends, he was sent to Vietnam, the war against the spread of Communism.

After serving three years in Hell, he returned home as Warrant Officer James Morgan, awarded the Victoria Cross for bravery above and beyond the call of duty. He felt this honor was undeserved but wore the medal as a constant and grim reminder of his friends and comrades who died in action.

Jim's marriage to Diana lasted eight years and produced a wonderful son, Jeremy, and beautiful daughter, Felicity. Constant flashbacks and occasional violent outbursts were both a legacy from the war and a danger to his family. So one day, after leaving a brief note to his wife, Jim simply packed a bag and left.

Family and friends judged him harshly for this, calling him an *asshole* and other derogatory terms for leaving his young family. There wasn't one day that passed, however, that he didn't feel guilty at what he'd done. Regardless, he felt it best at the time. He had undergone counseling for more than three months on his return from combat, but the psychologist had just enforced the feeling of futility and guilt at having engaged in the war. Any pride he may have felt at having fought for his country, evaporated. After each counseling session, Jim left feeling more depressed than before he'd gone in.

He had no hope of resuming his previous, promising career. Despite an occasional part-time job, he remained unable to land a permanent position due to his PTSD. Feeling depressed and worthless, he found solace in a bottle.

Each year on his children's and wife's birthdays, Jim would go out of his way to send cards. He'd even forgo his much cherished bottle of bourbon for that week so he could afford to buy Diana a bottle of what he remembered to be her favorite perfume, Tweed. It saddened, but didn't surprise him that there was never a reply. Besides, where would they send it, *No Fixed Abode*? Jeremy and Felicity would be grown now, probably with families of their own. He brushed away a tear as he realized he could be a grandfather and wouldn't even know.

Jim stood up, ran his fingers through his untidy hair, and ambled over to a nearby trash bin. Reaching in, he located a half-eaten hot dog and yesterday's newspaper, but his scavenging was rudely interrupted by a tall young police officer who exclaimed, "Okay, Pop, move along! The café's closed."

Stuffing what remained of the hot dog in his mouth, Jim folded the newspaper and placed it in his jacket pocket. He strolled along the pathway unconsciously obeying a sign that read, PLEASE KEEP OFF THE

36

GRASS. Now and then he would stoop to pick up a piece of paper or anything that caught his eye. Jim often came across small change, and once even found a twenty dollar bill with which he bought a trench coat at the Army Disposals. Besides, picking up rubbish helped to keep the park tidy. While he lived here it was the least he could do.

An attractive, young woman hurried past clutching the hand of a small boy whose short legs were forced almost into a run to keep up.

"Hurry up, Michael!" she scolded, "You're already late for school."

The boy's backpack slipped from his shoulder, slowing them down as he stooped to hitch it back up.

"But, Mommy, who's that man?" he asked inquisitively, pointing at Jim.

"Oh, he's just a tramp," she replied uncaringly, "Don't point, it's rude!"

Jim smiled as they passed and bowed slightly. He was used to such remarks.

"Just a tramp," he repeated quietly to himself as the woman and boy stopped at a kiosk near the park's entrance.

The Victoria Cross, which hung around his neck, is designed in the form of the Maltese Cross — in the center of the medal is a lion guardant standing upon the Royal Crown. The words *For Valor* are inscribed below. The Victoria Cross hung suspended from a crimson ribbon. On the reverse of the cross, the date of the act of bravery is inscribed, along with the name, rank, and unit of the recipient.

The woman momentarily let go of her son's hand to reach for her purse. Immediately, he was captivated by a flock of pigeons nearby.

Suddenly, she turned and cried, "Michael, come back!"

The boy raced after a bird, which now flew towards the busy street. He seemed oblivious to both the traffic and his mother's frantic screams.

Brakes screeched as Michael burst onto the busy road, but the car could not stop in time. As if from nowhere a powerful arm appeared, gripping the boy around the waist and pulling him to safety.

Jim had acted impulsively. In Vietnam quick reflexes were a necessity for staying alive. He had used them now to save a life.

The frightened boy was hugged by his distraught mother, "Oh Mikey, are you all right?" she sobbed.

Eventually realizing that her son wasn't hurt, but lucky to be alive, she turned to Jim.

"Thank you, sir, you saved my son's life," she said, genuinely thankful. "How can I repay you?"

Jim looked at them for a moment, a touch of nostalgia about his own family invading his thoughts.

"A buck for a cup of coffee. That'd suit me fine," he said, rubbing his whiskers nervously.

People began to crowd around the boy, and someone even bought him an ice cream cone. The driver of the car had recovered from his initial shock as well and was busy offering his sincere apologies. Then the young police officer, who had been taking statements, gave Michael a gentle lecture on road safety.

Crowds made Jim nervous, so he took the dollar, bought a cup of coffee at the canteen, and then quietly walked back towards the security of the park.

A news crew had finally arrived, and a reporter approached Michael's mother. "Excuse me, Madam, can you tell me what happened?"

"That man!" she replied, pointing after Jim. "He saved my boy's life. He's a hero."

The reporter wasted no time in pursuing the shabby hobo and bombarding him with questions. He saw the cross pinned to Jim's chest, and subsequently a headline appeared in the next day's Bulletin — "WAR HERO SAVES BOY'S LIFE."

Being a celebrity was not Jim's ambition, and he shunned further publicity. He refused to speak to another

38

reporter regarding the incident. Even a couple generous offers from magazines to buy his story were politely refused.

Life in the park soon returned to normal.

Sitting quietly on *his* bench, Jim unpinned the Victoria Cross and polished it on his sleeve.

"Maybe I do deserve you after all," he said with a grin, then re-pinned it on the lapel of his coat.

The End

About The Author:

John Hansen is a writer and poet who lives with his wife, Kathleen, on a rural property in South East Queensland, Australia. He is interested in the stories and lives of our servicemen/women and veterans from all wars.

John's father served in the navy in WW11, as did five of his uncles in various services and a cousin in Vietnam.

Just a Humble Hero was originally written as a poem titled *Just a Tramp* but turned into a story in the hope of reaching a wider audience.

You can visit John at *Poetry With Purpose:*
http://jodahkamah.wix.com/the-sleepy-poet

Dead Man Walking
by Robin Merrill

I am dead man walking, slowed to a dirge.
My clothes are heavy, I still scratch at bites,
from sand fleas long fallen, venom I can't purge.
No reason left in me, no remnant of fight.

I do not bother to learn new names.
I remember enough, my mind stopped up.
People walk past daily, they all look the same.
Each face is long dead, each a clink in my cup.

I wait for nature, haven't earned my escape.
I sacrificed my soul in the desert—it
waits there for rescue that is always too late,
weeping, gnashing, too thirsty to spit.

I hold my hands over a communal fire,
keeps me from freezing, keeps me a liar.

About the Author:

Robin Merrill is a writer, editor, and performance poet
from Central Maine. Her work has appeared in hundreds
of publications, and three of her poems have been
featured on *The Writer's Almanac* with Garrison Keillor.
Her newest collection, *Jesus Was a Feminist and other
poems*, is available from Moon Pie Press. She
represented Portland, Maine at the 2013 National Poetry
Slam and the 2014 Individual World Poetry Slam. Visit
her at: robinmerrill.com

To Grandpa Harris: a veteran, a father, a grandfather, and someone who left too soon before I could get to know him.

That Time We Brought Some Veterans Down to Mexico
by Evan Harris

We often hear about how we're supposed to act around our men and women in uniform: grateful, thankful, and appreciative. None of these things are untrue in the least, but many times, it can be difficult to walk up to a complete stranger, know nothing about them, and say, "Hey, thanks for your service." I've been around the military my entire life—my grandfather flew F-4's in the Vietnam War and later worked at the Pentagon, and my other grandfather was a paratrooper in the 101st Airborne Division. Even my brother served as an ROTC cadet in college. Being around veterans, hearing their stories, seeing how they coped after their service really wasn't something I ever thought twice about most times.

But here I am, sitting by the ocean in Mexico, nervous about meeting the veterans we'd brought down. How would they be? Would they be nice? Would they think me ungrateful? A torrent of thoughts ran through my head because most of us had never met any of these guys before.

Let me start by backing up a little. Every year, my family coordinates a large billfish fishing tournament in Mexico. And since its inception in the early 2000s, everyone in the group has collectively decided where to give some extra money on each trip. While most of the trip expenses are for chartering boats, room and board, and hats, we always put aside some money for some meaningful cause as well.

For a couple years, we gave a donation to an orphanage, another year we helped repair a pedestrian bridge on the highway outside of the town we stayed in.

43

Previous years donations had gone to melanoma research.

While all about relaxing, the trip included a strong element of charity and giving. The truth of the matter was that this tradition started because one of our relatives had passed away from melanoma, leaving behind his wife and two young children. The tournament, named after him, had also provided some extra charity money that had gone to the children's college funds.

But, as the fishing trip grew in size, so did a desire to give back even more. This fact once again brings me back to why I'm sitting at a beach bar on the Caribbean side of the Mexican coast. Months before, by luck, fate, or probably just over a couple of beers, some of the fishing trip organizers, A.K.A. my uncles and cousins, had befriended a veteran.

Either they got to talking about the fishing trip or the veteran, we can call him Jake, mentioned he was a member of this wounded veterans group. Regardless, the idea was born to bring veterans to the Mexico trip. This idea went beyond just inviting veterans down to come fishing. We wanted everything to be paid for—flights, hotels, dinners, etc. That right there would become a challenge all unto itself.

To set the scene, most of us hadn't realized that the charitable portion of the trip would go to bringing as many veterans down as financially possible. You have to understand that for this kind of trip, there is a good amount of preparation that starts five to six months prior.

Emails fly back and forth, flights are coordinated, and people brag about the fish they caught in years' past. Through these torrents of emails and smack-talking, most of the people going on the trip have no idea what the charity cause will be until a few weeks before. But a couple months out, we all got an email that said things were going to be a little different this year.

Most of the people going on the trip were already excited and looking forward to the warm Mexican sun and fishing in the blue waters of the Caribbean Ocean.

While there are a good number of people on the email chain when things are being planned, only a handful actively reply and email back before the trip. Luckily, getting that email saying that the group needed help paying for veterans on the trip pretty much blew the doors off of people responding. Getting these veterans to go on the trip mobilized everyone already attending to get the word out and donate money.

We all know that asking any audience for money is an acquired skill. And asking guys to give more money for a trip they have already paid a good amount of money to go on isn't always received with enthusiasm.

Frankly, that stereotype could not have been more wrong. No one going on the trip thought twice about giving extra money, or asking their company or friends to help donate money for these veterans. Long story not so short, the fishing group and some outside companies raised enough money to fully pay for seven veterans.

Again, here I am waiting to meet these guys, seven people who will be very different than the normal people who usually attended. The people who usually came on this trip did not differ too much—all family and very close friends. So, this change in attendees unnerved me. And as much as everyone on the trip grew excited to meet these veterans, it introduced a new dynamic.

These seven guys had either served time in Iraq or in Afghanistan, had probably seen some terrible things, and had fought in ways that most of us on this trip could hardly understand or handle. On top of that, each one of these guys were disabled veterans.

One guy had lost half of his leg, another had lost both legs, and another had been shot in the head. Nearly all of them had suffered and were recovering from PTSD. The list of injuries was intense, almost unreal. These men had experienced and survived combat and war. How could we hope to help them overcome all of the things they had been through, and all of the simple challenges they faced every day, with really no experience or knowledge as to what they had gone through or what they dealt with today?

Most of us know that people are amazing. Especially those experiencing intense trauma and loss, it is truly a blessing to see what people can go through and, despite it all, still turn out normal on the other side.

I remember seeing all of the veterans walk up to the bar on the first day of the trip. Me, my dad, and some family had been waiting for them, wanting to meet all of them before the fishing started. And more importantly, we just wanted to meet these guys and get to know them.

All of this anxiety about how our first introduction would go pretty much washed away like the tide instantly. Meeting those veterans on that Mexico beach the first day was just about as normal as meeting any group of friends for a drink at a bar in Mexico.

To this day, I still think about the positivity and just sheer joy these guys exuded. Most people are pretty good at reading other people's moods and body language, and so, at times, it isn't too hard to really understand a person's mindset or attitude as you talk. Not one guy complained or even became upset. Each had genuinely seemed to be in good spirits.

I think these seven veterans ended bringing some life into the party, as they were in better moods than most of the other guys on the trip!

I found that amazing because when I saw them, I immediately thought about what their day must have been like just to get to Mexico. I am a pretty healthy guy. I have all of my arms and legs, and consider myself pretty sound mentally, but after traveling all day, I am miserable to be around. Flying into another country, specifically Mexico, ranks as one of the most frustrating experiences ever. Even airports in the United States are no amusement park. The checking bags, security lines, security check, finding the gate, boarding the plane for an hour, waiting to get off the plane when it lands, baggage claim, customs, etc., can all wear on one's last nerve.

By no means an easy process, these veterans, guys with missing legs and arms, and other serious issues did it and had remained in a better mood then me! It's safe to say that these guys had an amazing outlook on life, an uplifting attitude that could not be matched. It definitely made the trip extremely special, I think, for most of the regulars that come every year, this fact became a real rallying point.

After the first day, the tournament got going pretty quickly. The basic schedule is: first day free, second day fishing in the morning, third day free day, and fourth day fishing in the afternoon along with the end of tournament dinner. Everyone usually flies home on the fifth day. The fees for the trip cover group dinners every night as well.

Unlike much of my family who live on the East Coast in Washington, D.C., I did not know many of these veterans, as they also lived in and around the Washington, D.C. area. As I got to know some of the veterans and their stories, it showed me again what it meant to move on from a difficult trauma.

One of the veterans, Jake, one of the first guys my family had met, had a pretty remarkable story. He was the veteran that had half of his leg missing. He had lost it while jumping over a wall and landing on a pressure plate that exploded while on patrol.

He had spent considerable time at Walter Reed Hospital, one of the main military hospitals in the United States. Now a successful entrepreneur, he had also married and had two kids. To be honest, he seemed just about the same as you and me. Clear as a bell, I remember the way he told the story about him losing half of his leg.

Me, and a few other guys on the trip floated in the shallow part of the bay near the beach as Jake described his injury and recovery in detail. An intense story, how calm and almost dismissive Jake spoke about the whole ordeal shocked me. He relayed the story to us as if some problem at work, or some other trivial thing.

Truth be told, I had played this scenario out in my mind several times before the trip. In my mind, I imagined one of the veteran's telling us this harrowing story about how they'd been injured, and it would be this intense ordeal during which he would remain stone-faced as he recounted what had happened.

Yeah, I'd been proven completely wrong about that one. Jake had obviously moved on with his life. This major, most likely life-changing injury while serving his country, had not removed his desire to live or enjoy life. You could read it, clear as a book, in the way he told the story.

Clearer than the Caribbean water we floated in, Jake had moved on from his disability and brushed it off. All of us stared blankly at the waves or the sky as he recounted details, but Jake could have been telling you about a trip to the grocery store.

Another great story about Jake really showed his resolve and how he, and pretty much every other veteran on the trip, had overcome their injuries. At the beach bar we always went to are these tall stools that face the ocean. As the veterans came around and introduced themselves to everyone, Jake had decided to sit on one of these stools.

Now, what is one of the worst things you could imagine happening to someone who has an artificial limb? If you said someone accidentally knocking it off, then you would be one hundred percent correct. And, that is exactly what happened. Jake sat on a stool with his feet hanging out and someone fell into Jake, knocking his artificial leg *off*!

It's Mexico. The sun shone, everyone listened to music and had been having a good time. I have never heard a place get so quiet in such a short amount of time. For a few seconds, I think most of us who'd witnessed what happened felt genuine terror. Was Jake going to flip out? Did this guy just ruin the trip? Do we grab his artificial leg and help him put it back on?

I immediately looked at Jake. Jake looked at the guy, and the guy who'd knocked his leg off turned transparent white. Then all at once, everyone started laughing. And, I mean everyone! It turned out to be one of the funniest and most memorable parts of the trip.

Truth be told, four days on vacation goes quickly. As I had been on this trip numerous times before, I knew what to expect from fishing for billfish and our fun group dinners at night. However, by the end of this trip, we knew that bringing these guys down to fish with us had been special in some way.

These veterans had overcome terrible injuries, injuries that probably could have killed them, along with mental anguish. These guys were heroes in every sense of the word. Not for the service they provided, but for the bravery and peace with which they lived with the challenges in their lives. One of the veterans, a double-leg amputee literally in the best shape of anyone on the trip, trained for the para-Olympics.

Another veteran, the one who'd been shot in the head by a sniper, proved himself one of the happiest and most gracious guys on the trip. That said something for a guy who had to wear a bib every time he ate because he still had trouble chewing normally.

As the trip wound to a close, by the end of tournament dinner, many of the guys on the trip had come to realize what a difference these veterans' presence had made. For the most part, the people who plan this fishing trip are actually my uncles and my father. One of the most sincere things I've ever witnessed had to be the head of the veterans group presenting all of them with *challenge coins*.

There were few times when the room of about forty guys got emotional, but that definitely proved one of them. It's hard to say that you can get to know someone over a couple day vacation. Many other times on the trip, I had met people and befriended them.

On the other hand, something about meeting and talking to these seven guys impacted me in a powerful way. There's a famous quote that goes along the lines of, *People say that motivation does not last. And neither does bathing, that's why we recommend it daily.* Joining with these veterans to celebrate their service, sacrifice, and ability to overcome their injuries was truly a life-changing experience that continues to provide motivation each day in how to be positive.

In this country, we have the blessing of an all volunteer military. The United States was founded by people who volunteered to fight for freedom, and our modern day armed forces are filled with people who have taken the oath to serve our freedoms and its' citizens. When men and women are deployed to active duty, they understand the service and sacrifice necessary to get the job done.

All of us pray that each one of our military service members come home safely. Still, we also know the reality of conflict and war, that it can leave long-term physical and mental damage in our veterans. While many of us may believe there is little that we can do to help once our veterans return home, nothing is farther from the truth.

I would have never believed that taking a bunch of veterans on a fishing trip to Mexico would have been meaningful in the long term. It was obvious that it was a great thing to do. Many people, myself included, had this idea that we were somehow doing these veterans a favor by bringing them. It's funny how things find a way of reversing themselves. They clearly did us the favor.

We hear so much about service, honor, and humility in regards to our heroes in uniform. Professional sports, businesses, and countless organizations go to great lengths to provide awareness and support for veterans, especially those who come home from war with physical and mental injuries.

Too few of us take time to hear these heroes, to talk to veterans and see how far they have come from a debilitating injury. The Mexico trip showed me that these veterans had kept fighting after their injuries, and that they had refused to accept their shortcomings. While I thought I was helping them out by bringing them down for a vacation, they actually did more for me and my family by showing us what it meant to get back up after you've been knocked down.

They showed us what they already knew from training and duty, that they could overcome any obstacle and defeat anything put in their path. As one of the guys on the Mexico trip said during the end of tournament dinner, "A nation who forgets its defenders will be itself forgotten." Our American heroes come in many forms, and their courage does not end when they take off their uniform. By recognizing their bravery and celebrating the strides of a successful recovery, we can better help veterans move on from the terrors of war.

The End

About the Author:

Evan Harris has written on veteran's issues for the California State Legislature, and has had many veterans' in his own family.

For Dad

Post-Traumatic Stress Disorder
by Gregory Roorda

The world is not as you left it.
When you do get back
To it.
It is not the same shape
Or color.
It does not feel
The same.
The world you left
Is gone.

But everyone keeps telling you
That it's okay.
Just take it easy
Give it some time.
Relax
Everything will be all right.

But you know differently.
You know you don't belong.
Not in this shiny bubble.
You know the truth.
You know how bad it can really get.
You know how bad people can really get.

Everything looks the same
But nothing is
The same.
Everything sounds the same
But nothing is
The same.

You never get back
To the world.
Not really.

About the Author:

Gregory Roorda was born in Detroit, Michigan. He spent six years in the United States Navy where he served in Operation Desert Storm. He has lived in California, Michigan, Texas, and Iowa. He graduated from Iowa State University with a Bachelors of Liberal Arts Degree. He is married and lives in Missouri.

I have always looked up to army men. The kind of selfless dedication they show for their country makes me bow in appreciation. I happened to chance upon one such person, Phil Dynan, who had joined the US Army Security agency and now works as a painter and serigrapher. His story inspired me, and this tale is dedicated to him. May you continue to inspire endless people like me.

The Demons Will Someday Die
by Shruti Fatehpuria

The sun slept, blanketed amidst the thick dark clouds. If you looked at the sky, you would find an eerie bliss. It seemed like the world slumbered lazily devoid of any worry. However, the irony proved too hard to take for Oliver.

He tossed and turned in his bed, a total of sixty-seven times. Call it OCD or whatever fancy biological term you prefer, but when peace didn't come he found an uncanny comfort in counting the number of times he tossed in bed.

Every day, he fell into the same routine. The numbers varied. Some days, he'd counted as low as thirty-three while his personal best score stood at one hundred and ninety-seven. That night remained the most tormenting of all.

Perhaps a trick of mind, but when you've been to the battlefield, you know not to take anything for granted. Life could change in the blink of an eye. He was proof.

As his eyes finally gave way to sleep thanks to the rhythmic sound of the rumbling water flowing beyond the little cottage that was home to none, he glided into the land of dreams.

A beautiful face with the most mesmerizing green eyes he had ever seen beheld his gaze. The face oddly comforted him. The more he looked toward it, the better he felt. However, short-lived comfort gave way to a loud sound. Somewhere from far and beyond came a noise that seemed to pierce his ears, and soon he found blood trickling from his forehead. The whole scene turned morbid with corpses lying around everywhere.

He woke up covered in sweat and panic. Nightmares. What is life but irony? The nation called him a hero. Was a hero supposed to wake up covered in sweat and scream in his sleep because the ghost of his past never let him be at peace?

So far, he had tried every single possible thing that he could for the sake of getting over his PSTD to no avail. Every day seemed to be worse than the previous one. He'd begun to contemplate if he would live the rest of his life being a slave to the days that had already passed.

As he mulled over these thoughts and tried to shrug off the remnants of his lost sleep, his phone buzzed. It always alarmed him to receive a call at such wee hours. Another memory came of his army camp where they expected calls at unexpected times. Anything could happen and often did. However, it had been three years now since he'd retired from the army. So, a call at four thirty in the morning pushed his panic button.

As Oliver sprang to reach his phone, his bad day got worse. Uncle Bradley, his only relative with whom he really kept some form of contact, had been diagnosed with cancer for the third time. The chances of survival very slim, Brad desired to see him one last time. He definitely didn't have the heart to say no to the man who'd loved him like his own child.

Hesitantly, he packed his bags as he ventured to the place that offered him some of the best memories of his life. On the road to Alford, Florida, he kept recollecting memories of the past—those blissful days when his soul hadn't been cursed with nightmares that woke him every night.

While he remained proud of serving his motherland, a part of him felt sorry for all those valiant soldiers whom he killed, the hapless women whom he widowed, the innocent children who'd lost their fathers, and those parents who'd lost their children. The guilt weighed too heavily on him when he thought of his own mates whom he'd lost. His heart shred to pieces. Who said a soldier was brave? A solider died every day, during the war and post war as well. Maybe staying at Alford, in the little place where he'd grown up, his heart would heal and his soul would once again smile. However, one very big *if* stood between him and his goal. Regardless, on he marched because as a soldier, he knew one thing. When time came, you always stood for the people you cared for, and Uncle Bradley had taught him more than his dad ever did.

****

As his flight landed in Florida and he stepped down, the air smelled of peace. He hugged the memories of the bygone times, of his careless childhood, like the echoing sound of his own laughter as many boys hung out together. Sometimes, he felt he needed to hug memories, to embrace them fully, to feel alive all over again.

He reached the little old cabin beside the seashore and peered in the gate.

"Uncle Brad, Uncle Brad. Hello, where are you?"

"In here," came a voice, which he heard like the songs of birds. The sound rang out so melodious that for a moment he felt all his nerves singing together.

"When did Uncle Brad get all feminine?" He chuckled at his own thought as he entered the room where the voice had come from.

As he sauntered in, he found a lady sitting beside the bed caressing the hair of what appeared an old, haggard man. It took him more than a few seconds to realize that the haggard man who had shrunken more than humanly possible, was none other than his very own ebullient Uncle Brad. In that instant, nothing else mattered as he quickly crossed the spaces between the door and the bed. He took his little Uncle into his arms.

"Ah, son, you are finally here," the old man sighed.

"Why didn't you call me sooner? You look terrible Uncle! What happened to Simon? Isn't he here with you?"

"You are not supposed to ask him so many things. He needs rest and lots of love and care," sang the lady sitting beside.

Oliver took a moment to really look at her. His heart felt torn at the sight of his Uncle looking so shriveled and tiny. He battled a disease that seemed hell bent on taking him down. Oliver's heart started beating too loud for his own comfort.

Her eyes shone the fiercest shade of green God ever made. She wore a blue top that did wonders for her cleavage. Her red skirt dangled at her knees. All the blood drained from his face at the sight of her legs. If he'd been an artist, he would've painted her and put Mona Lisa to shame! He found himself gaping and staring shamelessly at her, unable to even blink. She looked like a Greek goddess, only to him she appeared so much more!

What was the most beautiful goddess doing in his Uncle's cabin?

Before he could form a coherent response, she nudged him in the chest, "Mister, care to speak or are you going to just stare?"

"I... I... I am Oliver. Brad is my uncle," he found himself nervous and stuttering to form a coherent response.

Holy Lord, he couldn't remember the last time someone had made him nervous. Here he stood in the cabin where he'd spent a larger part of his childhood, blushing and shy, unable to even talk to a woman! How on earth had he become a teenager in a span of minutes?

Self-control had been taught with diligence at military camp, and so he chided his insides to behave.

With a fake stern look on his face, he murmured, "Now you, young lady. Tell me what have you been doing at my Uncle's cabin?"

"Oh finally, Oliver, you've come. Brad has been talking of you all day, every day, for a month. What took you so long, honey?"

She'd said quite a lot of words, but his heart had somersaulted at the word, *honey*. Sure, people in this small town of Florida used the word *honey* occasionally, but his heart was too loaded with hormones today. However, very reluctantly, he decided he was not here for a fling. His uncle had to be his focus.

So, he hesitated a second and then replied to the questions the girl in red had put forth. She in turn updated him about Uncle Brad.

Brad had been battling cancer for quite some time now. His son traveled for his job. He journeyed on year long escapades into unknown lands that were largely undeveloped. He could not be traced.

Oliver now had to take care of Brad. Since it had taken quite a lot of time to trace him down too, it was Estela, the girl with tantalizing long sexy legs, who'd decided to attend to him. Now that he was here, he wondered if Estela would leave. If so, the cabin would once again be cold as hell, just like he remembered it to be. Oliver got a really sorry look on his face as he fussed over these thoughts when someone nudged him hard in his ribs.

That girl knew how to hit!

"Honey, you seem to think more than an average man does in a year," sang Estela.

He gave a sheepish grin and said, "Your voice sings more than the nightingales do all their life."

At this, she laughed heartily. He knew the poets wrote about that sound in their love poetry. The room faded. Oliver only heard the melody of her voice. It sounded like the waterfalls had flooded with the symphony of a flowing river. He seemed to have come to life for once, but he felt like his time in Florida could be a lot of trouble.

Estela seemed like a girl that had trouble written all over her. Perhaps, it wasn't her. Rather, his little heart,

59

which he had fiercely locked inside, had started a revolution to come out and beat heavily.

"Stay safe. Stay away," he murmured.

Then he surprised both himself and her, as he planted one long kiss on her lips. At least she didn't hit him or hesitate. Regardless, an intensity built inside him, something much worse than being punched in the gut. What started as a slow, soft kiss ended up hot and passionate. Unable to withdraw himself, he kept going on and on until his lips burned.

"Shit," he murmured as he finally took leave from her mouth.

"Holy hell, what was that?" said Estela in response.

They both stared at each other. Estela blushed and opened her mouth as if to speak again, but she didn't.

Instead, Oliver barked, "I am trouble. Stay away from me. I am big trouble."

He didn't wait for Estela to respond before he marched out from the cabin into the dark, all the while cursing under his breath. He heard Estela curse as she stood in the doorway.

****

"What the hell does he think, kissing me, yelling at me, and then just walking out? What a jerk! Wonder why Brad wanted him to come in the first place? Absolutely doesn't seem like the guy Brad told me about," Estela ranted.

As she muttered and cursed at the man who had kissed the hell out of her, she absently found herself touching her lips as she relived that one kiss which had scrambled her brain, made her body tremble.

She went back inside the room so she could attend to Brad and maybe, a part of her wanted to know more about Oliver too. Now that they had kissed, she wanted to know why he was a trouble she couldn't handle.

****

He tried staying away, but Oliver could not resist the temptation that came in the name of Estela. Estela looked like a sin he wanted to commit. As they both worked together to help Brad recover, he bumped into Estela quite a lot. Trying to maintain his distance from her only made him crave for her even more.

After trying everything and failing, he finally confronted Estela.

"Hi," he offered with a hitch in his voice.

"Are you talking to me, mister?" she spat back, though without an edge to her voice.

"No *honey* for me today?" he attempted to tease.

"Are you talking to me, *honey*?" She met him tease for tease.

"Yes, as a matter of fact; I am!"

"Do you plan to kiss me and leave me again? If this is your plan, kindly excuse me, *honey*."

For the first time in the last ten days, Oliver realized how he'd unintentionally hurt her. He had never bothered to explain his actions. He mentally tried to frame an elegant response, but he found himself once again grabbing her by the hand and planting a full-length kiss on her mouth.

Estela stood firm, didn't move. About to retreat, she suddenly met him stroke for stroke. Soon they clung together. He found himself unable to catch his breath. The temperature in the kitchen soared higher than usual.

Estela broke the kiss and the silence muttering, "Shit?"

"My life is a total shit, Es. I am not the right guy for you. You don't want to waste your feelings on me. I am not here to stay. I'm here as long as Brad is. The very next day, after he's passed, I will leave and not come back again."

Estela looked into his eyes and poked him in his chest, "Who told you that I am here looking to get tied down to a guy? Let us have a fling for as long as you are here because you, mister, seem to be very uptight and need a girl like me to liven you up."

Before Oliver expressed his happiness and shock, she tiptoed over to him and planted one little kiss on his cheek.

61

She then murmured in his ear, "You are going to remember this time spent in Florida for a long, long time. Meet me for dinner tonight," she murmured seductively.

With this, she marched away singing, "Let's have a fling, babe," in her melodious voice.

Oliver McIrish, six feet four inches of sheer male perfection, ex army general, commander of a battalion in the Iraq war lost all his control.

"Women," he muttered, cursed and then smiled.

****

After spending close to three months in Alford, Florida, Oliver found Brad's condition deteriorating badly. The different rounds of chemotherapy had turned out to be useless. His hair had thinned so much that he barely had eyebrows anymore. He limped. There were signs daily, hourly, that his days were numbered. With no news of Simon, he saw longing in the eyes of a father to see his son for one last time.

Oliver desperately wanted to track down Simon. Despite having left the army three years ago, he could get the process running by calling in a few favors. He seldom wanted to use his resources, but he did this time for Uncle Brad. He had been the reason for the death of too many innocent souls. For once, he wanted to make one dying man happy.

He called his team who in turn contacted the other people needed. Soon, nearly thirteen men worked to locate a guy wandering aimlessly at a forlorn part of the world in search of bliss. It took a full three days for his rescue team to find the whereabouts of Simon.

He'd been last spotted at Ladakh, trekking in the wilderness of the Himalayas. The search team set out to let the guy know about the depleting health of his father.

Traveling all the way from Ladakh to Florida would take Simon a lot of time. Oliver could sense that time might play the bitch again. Uncle Brad inched closer to death every second. The news of Simon infused some life into him, but it seemed like his desire to see his only son again had intensified even more. If he died without

62

hugging Simon, Oliver feared his soul would never rest in peace.

He'd never felt so helpless in his life. He punched his fist in the wall and then threw a chair in anger. Estela inched closer, hugged him, and asked him to relax.

"We are all here to do our part, but destiny comes written in the stars. You did a noble deed. You are still a hero. You gave hope to Brad. You gave Simon a chance to see his ailing dad. Your heart holds a lot of love. You're an angel, honey," Estela offered.

He smiled and wondered how she saw the best in him when he was at his worst. He punched things and broke them and still she called him a hero. She didn't realize that he thought her an angel who'd showed him the beauty that life holds. However, he worried that his demons would be too much for her. The demons not only ate him up, but they could even feed on her soul. What had he been thinking, having a fling with a girl when he knew his heart a beast? Every night he woke up to sounds of canons tearing up bodies like they were toys. In the three months he'd spent here, he'd never spent a whole night with her. He remained afraid of revealing to her his true self, his true life. He never wanted her to see the coward in him that he did. War changed men. He was a beast—a coward fighting his own fears, a guy who hadn't slept once since the war had damaged him. He hated the man, the soldier he'd been who'd orphaned innocent children among other atrocities.

While serving in Iraq, a family had helped him, let him stay for the night when he'd gotten separated from his team. The woman of the family had served him food and offered him a bed to sleep in. She had attended his wounds, even when he had refused her attention.

He still remembered the way her eyes glimmered in the night as she had said to him, "I am a mother. For me, you are as much my child as my own son who is fighting for Iraq. I will weep if you go out and kill my son

63

tomorrow, but today, you are a child who needs my love."

It had killed every part of his soul when he'd opened fire a couple of days later on the same village where he had been granted shelter. The house where he had stayed blew up in flames. A son had failed because war never brings peace. This incident had forced him to consider giving up his army life, tired of being the reason for tears in too many eyes. The war in Iraq had left him devastated. He knew he could never give his heart because he no longer had it to give. Not really. Not fully.

The woman in Iraq's eyes kept coming back to him and all they did was murmur, *Son, you killed a mother.*

Suddenly, Oliver started sweating profusely in the middle of the day. Sure, these nightmares kept him company at night, but for the first time in three years since his therapy had ended, they'd come in broad daylight again.

At that moment, he realized, to him, Estela had grown into more than a simple fling. He had fallen in love with the girl. He couldn't. She would be the one he would damage. Thinking back to the angel mother in Iraq, he wouldn't chance killing Estela too.

Damaged people, damage people.

It had always been like that. The very thought of merely hurting Estela burnt his heart to pieces. No, he couldn't do that. He couldn't let his demons feed on the girl who was too beautiful to be engulfed by his evil soul.

He decided he had to leave before it got too late. Estella loved him. He knew that. He sensed it in the way she looked at him. Sure she realized he had his demons, all soldiers did. Yet, she didn't seem one to be scared away easily. Still, she could never know how deep his scars ran. The ghost of the war barely even let him smile. It had been foolish to think that love had the power to heal all parts of him. He still didn't sleep. The silhouette of the angel mother in Irag came up again.

"Son, you killed a mother."

64

He wiped off the sweat from his forehead. As Estela asked him what was wrong, he ran. Once a safe distance from her, he made an emergency call and arranged for a private flight for Simon. He avoided Estala as the boy flew all the way from Ladakh to Florida. Then, Oliver did what a coward would do. He left a note right before he ran away.

Dear Es,

I told you to stay away from me, didn't I? I am sorry for taking the coward's way out, but I have to go. You need to understand that I am damaged beyond repair. I have nothing in me to offer you. I know you love me. I could read it in your eyes. I felt it in your hugs. I tasted it in your kiss. However, I have a damaged heart that can't offer you the love you deserve. I have to go. Find a good guy who will give you the smile you need to wear.

Goodbye.

Ol.

He almost typed *Love You, Babe* at the end but knew it would be cruel to offer love and then take it away. No, he wasn't the guy for her. He was the one who'd killed the mom who'd fed him like a child. He would do the same to the Estela, kill her in some sense of the word even if not with a gun or bomb.

He couldn't bear the thought of being the demon again. She needed a civilian who led a normal life, who bought her pretty flowers all the time. She had no use of a man who never slept a single night, who woke draped in sweat, and who had befriended nightmares.

He knew Simon would make it. A part of him felt ashamed for not being there for Uncle Brad, but he knew there were better people around. Brad merely wanted his son, and he'd made sure Simon would be there. Whatever help Brad needed, he knew Es would offer. Nobody truly needed him. His presence and absence impacted no one except maybe Estela, but she'd get over it. He'd carry her in his dreams. Maybe, she

65

could've silence the nightmares inside, but maybe he was meant to live a life alone.
****
Eight years later.

Oliver came back home and found a letter on his table. A very rare sight, he hardly had any relatives who wanted to deal with him, let alone write to him. He preferred life this way. It meant he could do things his way without having to explain to anyone his long periods of absence.

As he opened the letter, he found himself drowned in too many memories. His cousin Simon had written to tell Oliver of his impending marriage. Who would have thought a boy so used to traveling on unknown expeditions would finally settle down in his life?

He almost dismissed the idea of attending the wedding, but found a little note that read,

Dad always wanted you to be my best man. I would have never hugged him if it hadn't been for you. His eyes scanned for you at the last moment. He told me, looks like God only wanted me to hug one of my two sons when I leave. Bro, he missed you very much. Come to my wedding. Be my best man. There is no one else who I would rather have than the man who loved my dad enough to help me cross continents to be there for him.

Miss you, bro,
Simon

His eyes moistened with tears. Brad called him his son. Somewhere in his heart, the realization that Brad had craved *only* for his son had pricked him, it had made him feel like an outsider. Little did he know that Brad loved him as much as he did Simon. It was foolish of him to walk away from his uncle for such selfish reasons when the man had needed him the most. While he tried very hard not to think on that time, the memories of a sexy lady who kissed him kept coming back to him.

66

Would Es recognize him? Was she married? Obviously, she wouldn't wait for eight long years for a guy who broke up with her in a letter. What if she had never gotten the letter? He hadn't even bothered to check up on her once he'd gone. It immediately stuck him that she might have left him an email. He'd often spoke to his uncle by way of emails as he never carried a mobile phone.

As he opened up his email, he found himself staring at a few thousand odd emails from various insurance companies, stress relief centers, therapists, veteran newsletters, and more. A laborious task, he fought his way through it. A part of him wished that Estela had at least tried once to reach out to him, that he'd mattered enough for her to bother to do so.

As he went through the mails in chronological order, he found one from her dated five years back. *She had tried.* She had missed him. He opened the email and read.

Ol,

It's been more than a couple of years now since you left me without a word. Like I told you, I do love you, but time taught me that you needed to move on. I would have waited all my life, if only you would have promised to come back. However, you never replied to my emails, which makes me wonder that perhaps you never did love me enough.

I am writing this email to you to let you know that I am going to marry. My husband trusted me enough to trust my love. Love is sometimes about trust and strength.

I am not timid, Ol. I know you were running from your demons, but I thought you were stronger than that. Anyway, what's gone is gone. I hope you all the best in your life, and maybe someday you will find a girl who could love you enough to force you to give your life one more chance. For us, this is the final goodbye.

Estela

He didn't have the heart to search for any previous emails. He knew they would be full of love and pleading to come back. He realized the damage he'd done when he'd left without a word.

His angel mother in Iraq had died because he'd been unable to stop the firing on an innocent place. His uncle had died without hugging him one last time because he'd been too scared to let his heart feel. The love of his life would marry another man because he'd been coward enough to walk away from her. The only person left was Simon. Regardless of what it took, one time, he'd be there for someone.

He packed his bags and headed to Alford. When he landed, he found a strange comfort in the air. Nostalgia hit him hard. The eight years he'd spent away melted into thin air. The memories he'd made during the three month long stay there eight years ago hugged him hard. He wanted to hug Estela, see his Uncle Brad and smack Simon on the back.

However, not all he wanted could be. He brushed away the tears that had fallen on his cheek and marched ahead so he could greet his cousin. He'd help him get on with a new life.

Simon had changed a lot since the last time Oliver had seen him. So, they caught up like old buddies did. Simon went on and on about how love had bound him down when he'd always thought being a free bird his destiny.

Oliver loved the chirpiness Simon had as he saw glimpses of his uncle in him. While he loved caching up with his cousin, his eyes scanned for the most beautiful pair of green eyes God had ever made. Among so many people at the home, his heart still felt lonely.

He chided himself for looking for Estela. She'd married to another guy. As he mulled over the thoughts, a little girl came up to him and tugged his trouser. He looked down and found another pair of beautiful green eyes staring at him. For a moment, he got lost in them. It reminded him of the first time he had seen Estela in this very home.

"Hey, are you a soldier? Someone said that you were a soldier. We've read about soldiers in school, and my dad was a soldier. Daddy never comes back home now. Do you know where soldiers go? Mommy says I ask a lot of questions," she chirped.

He smiled.

Before he could answer, someone from the crowd called for her, "Sara, come here. Mommy is looking for you."

He didn't need to turn back to find out who the voice belonged to. He'd know Estela's voice in a crowded room without even looking at her. However, as he turned back, he caught a glimpse of the woman who still ruled his heart.

They say people age with time, but if time had done anything, it had made her even prettier. Her cheeks appeared fuller. Her body looked a little curvier, but it made her look sexier. He fought to keep his thoughts under control. He reminded himself the woman was married. His gaze instantly went to her finger. Surprise caught his breath to find the ring finger devoid of a ring. His heart screamed. However, it seemed impolite to bring it up the subject, to ask why no ring, in their first conversation in eight years.

****

Estela stood there, transfixed to a single spot. That one man who'd left her without so much as a word stood in front of her. She stared as she recollected the memories that kept drowning her. *Oliver*, the name hung in her mind. She remained lost in a sea of emotions.

He left you without a goodbye. He never answered your emails. He will leave again. Don't talk, she mentally instructed her heart.

All of her instructions melted in a puddle of love when he simply uttered her name.

"Es, where's your ring?"

69

It took a moment for her to comprehend that he had actually read her email and still had not bothered to reply. Anger bubbled inside of her. She found herself turning bitter.

"I guess, sir, it is none of your business," she muttered, and stomped out of the room taking her daughter with her.

When she turned back, she failed to control the tears and her daughter exclaimed, "Mommy, why are you crying?"

Oliver flew across and took Estela's arms. She broke down with his touch. He guided her outside to the garden and asked her to rest on a chair.

He brought her water to drink and asked his cousin to take care of her daughter. When he turned his attention back to Es, she continued to cry, breaking into uncontrollable sobs.

"What happened, Es? I am sorry. I was a jerk. I shouldn't have asked about the ring. I only read the email the day before my flight here and found you had married. How is your husband? Your daughter said that you'd married a soldier?" He stumbled over the words.

"Yes, I did and he died. I am widowed."

****

Stunned silence surrounded them. Too much information floated through Oliver's mind to process. A widow. He knew at that instant that he had never loved another woman as fiercely as he did this one. However, the silhouette of war memories lurked in the background waiting to steal any ray of happiness that could light up his life.

He used to be a brave boy who'd fought against all odds. So why now as a man could he not fight his own demons?

As he looked at Es, love with its magic healed wounds that ran deeper than even he could fathom.

The End

A Message From the Author

In my mind, Oliver and Estela eventually got married. With Estela's unwavering love and support, Oliver returned to therapy. He found the more he shared about his experiences in Iraq, the more he healed. Estela also had the strength to listen to his horrible tales, and the way she counseled him, with love, from her heart, had made his nightmares slowly ebb away. Sleeping with the woman he adored and having her enveloped in his arms, brought him back to life more than anyone could ever know. Sure there were a few occasional days when he woke up covered in sweat, but Es seemed to just instinctively know how to comfort him.

A war never brings peace, especially not to the soldiers who fought in it. No one really wins when a battle is fought. If only the world realized this simple fact, there would be a lot less damaged souls. Not every soldier is gifted by life to have an Es nurse their wounds, and even those who do, sometimes it just isn't enough to heal what is broken in them no matter how hard those who love them try.

Just remember, no matter what your circumstances, a soldier is brave, and all you have sacrificed appreciated.

About the Author:

In a world, where almost everyone is striving to stand out by outdoing the other, Shruti Fatehpuria aims at merely finding her own place in the crowd. A software engineer by education, she made the choice to quit the suffocating clutches of the corporate world and embrace the comfort of pens and paper.

She works as a full time freelancer but amidst a tiring myriad of endless deadlines, she often takes out time to write so that she can satiate her unquenchable thirst to vent the inner feelings. An avid blogger, she nurses the

71

belief that life always wears too many shades that are blended into each other. The real journey that truly defines a story is to unveil all the shades that make us.

She is still not done with her part of the journey because there are more shades than she knows. However, sometimes it is the journey and not the destination that matters. She is in the quest to find her own story so that one day, she could read it and paint her own canvas of life but until then, dreams and reality share separate space.

For you, Dad. Recently gone, but never to be forgotten.
You taught us about unfailing compassion and love. I will
always be driven by the desire to share that love with
others. Thank you for making life precious.

To Love Again
by Anita Stienstra

"Our pleasant vices make instruments to plague us."
King Lear

Every morning I pray for my future husband.
Tomorrow continues to charm the hopeful even when
the past plagues today.
My first husband died in a car accident, left me with two
kids.
The second loaded bombs in the Middle East in the
1980s,
became a wanderer, sky diver, yogi, salesman, step
dad,
and then died from complications of advanced MS.

Two soldiers folded a flag in slow motion.
On his knees, my son placed it in my hands.
My son thought the Army was the only way
to pay for a college education he still doesn't have.
Working fulltime at a reserve center, he says they're
cutting his job.
Like me, my son and daughter are grown and alone.

Every morning I pray for my future son and daughter-in-
law.
I prayed for you even though I didn't know your name.
We've been pulling our bootstraps up for a long time.
But what else is there to do? We try so hard to live
all the words my son tattooed on his arms—loyalty,
respectfulness, and service. Yet, yesterday holds us
down.

73

I wish I'd prayed harder and longer. Maybe I didn't pray
right.
I wish I'd prayed more for complicated injuries,
for the ones that make you feel like I felt
going back to work after my husband died. Days of
trivial and ridiculous time spent pushing useless info
in an office while folks drank expensive coffee and spoke
of TV shows.

I wish I'd prayed more for you, nephew, who served
three duties
on the ground in Iraq and Afghanistan. For you,
my daughter's recent breakup, almost husband who
fought in Iraq.
Both with PTSD. Both with suicide stalking their solitude,
the silent boa that made my almost grandkids' father
leave my daughter right after they realized they loved
each other.

Maybe love has become as elusive as peace. And,
there's no
prosthetic for the heart. So…on I go and pray for those
who serve…
for those who might share the future with us…for life
itself
to be less cruel…for our choices to be less
senseless…for courage
to always believe that what we give means more than
the things we lose.
And, for a world where you and I can, and do, love
again.

About the Author:

Anita Stienstra of Phoenix holds a BA and MA in English
with a focus in poetry and poetics. She is publisher and
editor of Adonis Designs Press and an annual
international teen poetry and art anthology, *Navigating*

the Maze. She has read her poetry extensively at events and venues in central Illinois, taught writing at two colleges, wrote for newspaper and television, and facilitated several writing workshops. Awards received include John Knoepfle Creative Writing Award for Poetry, PWLF Presidential Award, Springfield Area Art Council Artist Advancement Award, and an Athena Award nomination from the Springfield Chamber of Commerce. Her work can be found in reviews, newspapers, anthologies, and also in six chapbooks.

Life is sometimes an unexpected journey. I dedicate this story to my husband, Mark, and his journey to recovery and finding the gifts God has blessed him with. Love will find a way.

Journey of a Hidden Life
by Julie Seedorf

The year was 1970. Young and enjoying life, I met the man of my dreams, or so I thought. He was fun, exciting and handsome. It wasn't love at first sight. Maybe that should have been my first clue, that if I continued on pursuing a relationship with this person it might lead to uncharted waters in my life. But then, isn't that what relationships are, uncharted waters?

The first time I met the man that was to be my husband he was a little too happy-go-lucky for my taste. By that I mean, he'd had too much to drink, but a friend had persuaded me to go with them for the evening. This friend ended up abandoning me with this jolly, easy-going, inebriated person. I wasn't impressed. I didn't like him. A few weeks later we met again. This time I saw him in a new light. Sober, fun, and charming this time around, I fell hard for him.

Maya Angelou has a quote that I think about often. It is "*When someone shows you who they are believe them; the first time.*"

The man who was to become my husband had recently returned from the war in Vietnam. In the days of this unpopular war, he'd returned home like many without fanfare. Quiet about his role in the war, I knew Mark had nightmares. He didn't even tell me he'd served in B Company, 2nd Battalion, 5th Cavalry, 1st Air Cav Division. I didn't find that out until this year. He didn't tell me attending a fireworks display would send him diving to the ground. He didn't tell me he'd had malaria, ring worm, kidney problems, etc., while serving in Vietnam. In fact, he didn't talk about it at all.

Being young and not fully understanding the repercussions of what war does to a person, I didn't question his silence about his time served. That is where Maya Angelou's statement haunts me. When I first heard that statement I thought that it explained my confusion. My husband had showed me who he was early on in our marriage, and I'd ignored what I saw. I put the blame on me—not being a good enough wife, mother and housekeeper.

I didn't think it had anything to do with the war. I blamed the alcohol. He had a drinking problem. I blamed myself. I should have known this when I married him. The signs were all there, but you know what they say about love being blind.

When our first son was born, at the birth Mark told me he was glad our hospital didn't let father's be present in the delivery room yet, because he wouldn't be able to be there. He knew he wouldn't be able to stand seeing someone he loved in pain. I remember spending most of the time in the hospital alone. The night before I came home from the hospital Mark had celebrated so much that he spent the night in his car. Of course, he didn't remember why. Sometimes he was happy when he would drink, and other times he would have terrible mood swings. I blamed the alcohol, his friends and myself. He came from a family that had trouble with alcohol. So, of course, that was the reason in my mind that he drank so much. All these reasons kept him in the bars and away from home. For part of my marriage, I spent my time chasing after him in the bars, putting my energy in getting him to come home and putting our children second.

Years passed, and we still didn't talk about the war. During one of my cleaning missions, I found pictures from his time in Vietnam stashed in the closet, hidden. Anything to do with the war, he avoided it, and that included friends he had served with.

As the years progressed we had another son and daughter. It was clear he loved his kids, but it was also clear that his time spent with the bottle was very important to him too. He held part of himself away from us. He always managed to hold a job and always provided for us financially.

At one point, I put myself in Co-Dependent Treatment to deal with my emotions and get myself the emotional help to deal with the drinking. At that time we'd thought Mark had quit drinking because we never saw him take a drink. Only, he was just a master at disguising his problem.

Over the years along with alcohol, my husband had dealt with depression, mood swings and angry outbursts. I contributed it to the alcohol. A few months after 9/11 I received a phone call late one afternoon. It was Mark. He'd had an accident. He told me that he was sitting in someone's car waiting for the police. I'd wanted to come, but he told me to wait. Then I received another phone call. Mark had been arrested for drunk driving.

The entire family rallied around. By his own choice, he decided to go in for treatment. Relief came. Finally, the man we loved would get the help he needed for his alcohol problem. We all participated in the family night and educational evenings. After treatment, we continued on with the aftercare and AA meetings. He started talking to his kids, and it appeared that the demons that seemed to haunt him were better.

During that time one my customers came to talk to me about my husband attending a support meeting for Veterans with PTSD. I dismissed the idea because his problems were caused by the alcohol and not any Post Traumatic Stress Disorder. He was getting better, and our lives were finally going to be normal. I was going to have an energetic, sober, caring and happy husband.

During his period of treatment my husband lost his job. I didn't worry. He always provided an income to support us. Mark decided to take a year to get his life together. The year went pretty good. As time wore on though, the depression started. Looking for a job proved stressful. When he finally found a job, it was a self-motivated career, and he couldn't seem to find the right level of motivation. He found another job he liked that paid minimum wage and commissions, but was let go after nine months. He picked up a bad bug and ended up getting a penicillin-induced superbug. This laid him up for months. The depression worsened.

I would go to work in the morning and leave my husband lying on the couch, to find him doing the same thing when I came home. Summers were better because he could get out on the golf course. Eventually, the doctors put him on anti-depressants. He took them for a while, but then quit because he thought himself better, that he didn't need them. Then, he would sink back into depression again along with mood swings that came with quitting the meds.

I had thought life would be better, would be more normal. What is that anyway? I thought we would finally have that happily ever after. The drinking stopped but the depression, mood swings and anger got worse.

One night I received an email from a gentleman living in Massachusetts looking for my husband. Apparently this gentleman's uncle had been in the same division in the service as my husband, and he was looking for men that had served with his uncle. I checked with Mark, but he would not talk or email with this man. He got very agitated talking about connecting with him at all. I asked if he recognized the name, but my husband informed me he didn't know any last names of anyone he served with. I let it go and answered the email myself.

The gentleman wrote back. He emailed me a link to a website about a battle my husband had been in. My husband had only ever mentioned one battle to me. I remembered that he'd said, "Have you ever thanked God the sun came up in the morning?" Sure, now the article spoke about this same battle, I started to understand the horror that he had went through.

I asked him about this battle, and he broke down and cried. He said, "Have you ever told your friends to go to a spot and then watch them be killed?" That was all he said. At that point, I knew it was more than the alcohol that had shut down the way this man lived his life. This was forty years after I met him.

I am a believer in God. This is where I believe God entered in and sent me help. The wife of a customer of mine stopped in one day and told me about her husband. He was getting help for PTSD. At that time, we were getting no help from the VA. We hadn't tried. My husband avoided the VA along with belonging and being active in any service groups. I never questioned his avoidance. Now I know, any activity would have served as a reminder of the past. We all, as a nation, let down the Vietnam Veterans when they came home from the war, and so they felt ashamed talking about their service.

A few hours after my customer left, her husband called me. He gave us the name and the location of whom we should contact. After much nagging and many cancellations of appointments, we did call the VA. Still, my husband didn't bring up his anxiety, his depression, or his inability to keep a job. He didn't mention how he couldn't participate in life or even care about other people. His physical needs were addressed but not his mental needs. He didn't share them with the doctor.

Finally, a wise Veteran's Service officer, after spending time with my husband, urged Mark to talk to someone about PTSD. Our kids also got involved and advised him to get help. He was finally diagnosed just this past year with PTSD and has begun treatment.

That's my part of his story leading up his diagnosis. I can't tell you about it with any depth when it comes to how he feels about his journey or his diagnosis, because you see, there is no magic cure. There may never be. He may never be any different. Spending time with his therapist or even at the clinic seems to lay him up on the couch for days. The war he fought changed him for life, and the older he gets the more it seems to affect him. I can't tell you why.

81

Here is what I can tell you. I'm going back to Maya Angelou's quote: "*When someone shows you who they are believe them; the first time.*" Years ago when I heard that quote, I believed that Mark had shown me who he was, and that I hadn't believed him. I was wrong. I don't believe Mark showed me who he was because he didn't know. What happened to him in his youth and in Vietnam changed him. It left him with a sense of loss so deep that he lost himself. I think in some way that is still true today all these forty-three years later.

A friend of mine told me what a relief it was for her husband to be diagnosed with PTSD, to know he wasn't crazy. I knew what she meant. Living with someone with PTSD makes us all feel we are crazy. None of us were crazy, we just exhibited crazy behavior because we didn't understand what was happening. I realized that nothing I did or did not do had caused any of the angry outbursts that seemed to come out of nowhere. I did not cause the drinking. I was not the true cause of the temper, the depression or the isolation.

I have heard people say that you choose your behavior. You do to some extent, but I believe there are times when someone with PTSD has no control over that behavior. The disease takes over. Unless they have the tools to manage it, they are lost.

Our children always knew they were loved, but there was a distance in the relationship with their father that could not be bridged. The distance got worse after the drinking stopped and after 9/11. The crutch that Mark relied on, the alcohol, to help him get through social situations and give him a boost in confidence to communicate, was gone. The drinking made him social and gave him coping skills. Sobriety pulled him closer to himself inside and made him a loner with his memories.

My husband is a good grandfather to his grandchildren. He is at his best when he is with his grandchildren. He shows them a side of himself that he never showed to us.

Our journey is not over. Our journey with PTSD is not easy. The diagnosis came as a relief because there are now glimmers of hope. We now know where to take the problem. And, as a family, we know it is an ongoing work in progress.

Mark is now sharing his Vietnam pictures with his grandchildren. He even tells them a few stories about the countryside of Vietnam. He is making an effort to reach out to his children, and he is making an effort with therapy to control his temper and to share who he is. Hopefully, he will get more involved with other veterans and spend time with friends again.

I have often asked myself how I signed on for this crazy life, and why I stayed. It has not been easy. I have shed many tears, and I still do. Yet, there is something about those vows *for better or for worse* that has kept me here. Since the PTSD diagnosis, I get the fact that Mark is not the person he wants to be, and that it is a struggle for him to get past the journey he lived in Vietnam. It was a journey of decisions and actions he would have never chosen had he never been put in the situations he was. It changed him. He lost himself, and he has not yet found who he wants to be. If he has at all, he doesn't know how to get there while still living with those memories.

This story is being shared with Mark's permission, and that in and of itself says he is making progress. I shudder to think where we would be without the diagnosis and people that understand what that diagnosis is and how to treat it. We, as a family, are grateful. As for the future, all we can do is love Mark as he is, as a husband, as a father and as a human being. Love will find a way along with the VA.

The End

About the Author:

Julie Seedorf is a freelance writer, columnist and Cozy Mystery Author. She has lived her life as a wife and mom, experiencing various careers including that of computer technician. Retiring from her computer repair business in January of 2014 to follow her dream, she transitioned to that of full-time writer. Outside of writing she likes to read, try new hobbies, and scurries to keep up with her social media. She lives with her husband and has two shysters of her own, Borris and Natasha. Her favorite moments are those she spends with her friends and family, especially her grandchildren.

You will find Julie at http://www.julieseedorf.com

I dedicate this poem to all those who suffer unjustly, soldiers in the military and in life. I want to especially thank Walter Tarwacki, my friend and mentor who served in World War II. I also want to thank all my friends who were loyal and stood by me, all my editors, and my grandma, P.D. Silk. I love you, grandma! Thanks for all your prayers and encouragement in my career! Love, Liberty.

She - A Brutal Truth
by Liberty Samantha Michael

She, the soldier came home
But she never truly returned
Nothing remains the same on peaceful soil
She left large parts on the war torn land
She wonders that if they saw her they wouldn't
understand

Day after day, night after night, things have changed
She no longer fights man
She fights herself
Disconnected
She longs to stay in seclusion now

She knows not what to do with the hatred
People gossip about her to explain what they can't
understand
At times amusing to overhear, other times it drives her to
rage
Her anger scares people who can't comprehend

It scares her too
She worries it could seem aimed at someone else
The counselor unintentionally creates an *I'm sick* or *I'm crazy* label
She sometimes get too close to people, then has to run
away

Happy just being on her own she finds herself gone for
several months
No point trying to talk when they can't see the real her

She misconstrues their concern
She wonders if they'll think she's done something wrong
She ponders they could think her antisocial
She's not going to their parties, so they'll think her a
traitor
Or worse that she's not there for them

She screams to God, "But who's here for me?"
Some treat her like trash on the street
They can't even look at her
They've called her a fiend and spit at her
They assume she's on drugs because she acts so
nervous at times

She runs around back and forth
She sits for a second, then she stands
She sits again, then she runs
She's confused about what to do
She wonders who she is, and she worries who she can
trust

She sometimes feels like she's not even in her body.
She feels like she's in a foreign land.
She wishes only for someone to reach out a hand
The government doesn't help and the disability check
isn't enough
She can barely survive

She wants to rise above and do something with her
wasted life
Yet, what can she do when she's always in fight mode?
She wonders who will be here to love and support her
She only needs some understanding and
encouragement

She doesn't need empty gestures, something that
makes them feel better
They can't throw money at her and expect her to get
better

She knows they have to work together

About the Author:

Liberty Samantha Michael is a Warrior—An East High
School Alumni with a Masters degree in writing. Having
enlisted in the army herself, veterans hold a special
place in Liberty's heart, as she feels their pain and wants
to help them.

Raised on The Lower East Side of Erie, Pennsylvania,
Christ unshackled Liberty from the life she endured
there. She had to rise above what she saw and become
brave in sharing her testimony through writing in the
hopes of helping others overcome some of life's more
tragic hardships as she herself did.

Having been published in such places as "The War Cry"
(Salvation Army magazine) and Erie Times News, as
well as websites like Wonderfully Woven and Erijams (as
Heather Dalrymple), Liberty finally feels empowered to
achieve her lifelong goal of helping others through her
gift of writing. "We don't have to suffer in silence, we can
collectively raise our voices and empower those who feel
they don't have a voice." Liberty says.

Liberty can be reached at godlyrenegade78@yahoo.com

Dedicated to my family. I love you. And to the men and women who selflessly serve others, may God bless you always.

The Mind of a Shrimp
by Robert E. Bergmann

A gradual morning is upon the pier. Sounds of nature whisper over the bay, while the sun strains to break the fog. It's a thick haze that bonds the division of sea and sky. The rising tide pushes the marshes scent of fresh salt into my lungs. I light my cigar and follow a Blue Herron floating across the sky. It's been over six months since my year in Afghanistan, but I still prefer these moments of loneliness. Since this last deployment, I've noticed my tolerance for other people's ignorance to be very shallow lately.

I hear the rumble of a weathered, mid-seventies pickup. It has worn tires, a scratched bed, and faded, baby blue paint but still hums the song of a well-maintained engine. In the cab I see the shadow of an elderly man cast his judging eye upon me. He passes words to the boy before pulling away. Wearing tethered overalls and seasoned Kmart special sneakers, the child strolls my way with a cooler in tow; he can't be more than twelve years old.

He nods a respectful "Gud mawnin sar," taking caution not to make eye contact for too long. He positions himself near one end of the ashen dingy dock, and tosses his shrimp net with precision.

I wish I had a camera.

It's one of those scenes that could never be fully captured by film. He draws in his net and shakes the catch onto the dock. While gathering the shrimp into the cooler, he uses peripheral to see if I'm watching. Again the net goes out with exactness, and again he watches me from the corner of his eye. His face reveals no emotion and I can't determine if he is waiting for my approval or worries of my authority.

89

Another cast.

Another catch.

This time he sees my smile. He knows I'm impressed with his skill, and that's the icebreaker he's been searching for.

While drawing in the net of another cast, he speaks without looking my way. "Dat seegar smells vary gud, sir."

"It tastes very good," I reply.

His comeback takes me by surprise.

"You wouldn't happens to has anotha you could spare?"

"No, sir, this is the only one I've brought," I say, while wondering if I did have another would I actually consider giving it to a boy of his age.

"You throw that net pretty well," I tell him.

"Yas, sir, me's pappy showed me how when I was a boy. You wanna try?" he asks.

I set my cigar and pen down, and tell him growing up in New York we didn't have fresh shrimp. He nods, hands me the net, and shows me how to hold and throw. I toss it and watch it never open, but make a tight thud, like a flat paddy hitting the water. I pull it in and continue to proceed with the lesson. After many attempts, it feels a little easier and finally starts opening. On my eighth or ninth toss, a single shrimp appears in the catch.

He holds it up and says, "Dat's yours, sir."

I say, "Yes it is, but go ahead and put it in your cooler."

He gives me a sideways look, and then tosses it back to the sea.

When I ask why, he tells me, "Pappy says it ain't right to eats anotha mans ketch."

I thank him for the training and give the net back. As I turn away, he asks if I'm a Marine. I look back and confirm I am. His eyes stay towards the sea, as the conversation carries.

"Did ya haves to goes to war?"

I tell him that I just got back from Afghanistan.

His face drops down, and I sense a bit of sadness.

"My olders brother was over there...thank you for servin, sir."

I gaze in silence, scared to press the topic any further.

"Thanks again for the lesson," I say, leaving the boy to his thoughts and duties.

While re-lighting my cigar, I see an oversized new 4X4 arriving. A young Marine and even younger girl get out. They carry a Wal-Mart shopping bag and a shiny new cooler. Her youthful skin is smooth and tan. Daisy Duke cut-off jeans, cowboy boots, and blond hair flowing from a ball cap give a flirty attractiveness. If her IQ is low, she doesn't need to worry, I'm sure all the boys get dumber in her presence.

My assumption increases as I see the guy proudly wearing a Lynyrd Skynyrd T-shirt, and a camouflaged ball cap on backwards.

He loudly says, "Good morning, sir."

I nod while drawing on my cigar. The young lady flashes a practiced smile, locking her eyes with mine.

"It's our first time," she says with a giggle, informing me of the obvious.

After passing by, she glances over her shoulder to ensure her backside didn't go unnoticed. The Marine's backwards ball cap has a confederate flag contrasting off the cammie background.

I hear her say, "I wonder what he's doing?

"Shut up. He's probably an officer," the young Marine says in a demeaning tone.

She flashes the kitten smile again. I've become the prey in a hunter's iron sights. I'm old enough to be her father and feel shameful for momentarily succumbing to her youthful bloom. They take their place at the opposite end of the dock, making me the midpoint between the skilled boy and the ignorant couple. It's not fair for me to make such an opinion of them, but as the Marine Corps teaches: first impressions are the strongest.

91

They pull a new net from the bag and study the single page, three step direction sheet. Again she giggles, a smirk in my direction, obviously confused by the comprehensive level of instruction. I watch as his first cast duplicates my own paddy-like splat. His face reveals instant frustration when he draws in the empty net.

Again, he throws with no avail.

By the third impatient cast, he starts decomposing with irritation.

She teases at me again, obviously piercing his spine of pride, "Looks like McDonald's for supper tonight."

With no preparation, he tosses the net again, this time adding a grunt of force. It doesn't open. Her eyes rapture my way.

I tell them they might want to ask for a free lesson, cocking my head toward the other end of the dock.

The boy continues to throw and catch with consistent accuracy. I know he is watching, though his face and eyes indicate otherwise.

Instantly my muscles tense as I hear the young Marine grumble under his breath, "No way I'm gonna ask a black boy for help."

He actually used a racial slur reserved for the truly ignorant with polluted hearts that doesn't deserve repeating here. But, that one word, one that linked the ignorance of the two using it, served as a trigger snapping my thoughts back into another time.

The angst takes me there again.

It's been a year but the memories of the deployment are fresh.

I was in the control tent of the "Skid Kids" helicopter squadron. An overweight gunny stood at the counter. His flight suit rolled down revealed an unwashed, salt-stained green tee shirt that indicated his lack of pride. I recognized the young captain on the other side of the counter. I'd been told he's one of the best pilots they have, and his clean appearance and educated demeanor enforced the professional tone in which he carried himself. He maintained composure, though frustrated with the lackadaisical attitude confronting him. He wanted his aircraft ready, but wasn't experienced enough not to press issues with the Marines of Maintenance Control. He thanked the Gunny and asked to be informed as soon as the bird was up.

"Oh, yes, sir, anything you need, sir," the gunny said with a hint of mockery that couldn't be proven but added salt to the Captain's irritation.

The Captain had moved barely two steps out of the tent when the Gunny told the young Lance Corporal next to him, "I can't stand the way black officers use their rank to get respect."

Again, he used that horrible racial slur that had brought my mind back here to this moment.

The younger Marine had said nothing, but his face showed him once again let down by his boss' contrast to the teachings of a drill instructor. The Corps imparts everyone green, but unfortunately racism slimed through the cracks at times. Not right, I rose to correct the scene. I knew my words would be lost on the gunny, but the Lance Corporal needed to see that this would not tolerated. I'd spent the night before sleepless in a sweat soaked cot, and now the discomforts of war would be released on a deserving target. I could only presume the Warrant Officer nearby to be too engrossed with the aircraft readiness report to catch the cause of my rage.

Before I spoke a word the "TIC" alarm sounded. "Troops In Contact" meant we had frontline ground Marines in need of immediate air support. The Captain crashed back in, frantic for a ready aircraft. Simultaneously, the Warrant Officer flew from his chair directing the Captain to his aircraft, and pressing the gunny with closed fists. The rest of the tent had been directed to leave as the Warrant Officer slammed the gunny through the plywood wall that held the dri-erase aircraft tracking board. Outside, it didn't take but a moment for the Captains new "Yankee" model Huey to

93

catch up and blast past the already in-route "Cobra" helicopter.

Two days later, a lieutenant came to the squadron with a sergeant by his side. They were looking for the Captain. I took them to the ready room and introduced him.

"Good morning, sir, I'm Lt. Goodwin, and this is Sgt. Jax," the Lieutenant said.

The Captain shook their hands and greeted them as if they were long lost brothers.

Before anyone could say another word, the sergeant blurted a thank you and embraced the Captain in his arms. Confused, the Captain looked at the lieutenant who had become the focus of everyone in the tent.

"Sgt Jax requested to thank you in person, sir. It was his squad you rescued two days ago," the Lieutenant stated.

"We didn't have a chance, and you saved us all," the Sergeant said.

"You saved us," he said again with another hug and tearful eyes.

The captain took it all in humbly, and with dignity directed the honor to his door gunner and the rest of the members of the squadron. Alcohol is not permitted in the combat zone, but that didn't prevent two six packs from being pulled from the sergeants backpack filled with rapidly melting ice—a gesture of sincere appreciation shared by Marines of all ranks.

The pitiful flopping sound of a net brings me back to the present.

The young girl continues to smile in pursuit, entertained by her fumbling boyfriend. She presses him to ask the boy for help. Watching again, the young black man adds more shrimp to his cooler. Resentful beyond any level of self-control, the marines ego heaves out a pissed off toss of the net. He watches in disgust as the net sinks. Absorbed by anger, he allowed the retention line to go with the net, lost with any hopes of fresh catch for evening supper.

94

The young black man never indicates any emotion as he glimpses at me with content in his eyes. I hear the blond laughing as she informs the ignorant boyfriend of his *jackas*s title.

Empty cooler in hand, he storms back to his truck without saying a word.

Indifferent to his anger, she follows.

Walking past she says, "I hope to see you again," sending a last chance glance of desperation.

Their truck isn't even out of sight as the experienced shrimper walks to where the couple stood moments ago.

I watch as the professional casts another perfect throw and draws up the Marines new net in his catch.

He walks past, beaming a smile and tells me, "My best ketch eva."

My cigar is near its end and the sun is finally expelling the fog with a warm brightness over the water. I see a light grey dolphin break the surface nearby, and then a dark porpoise follows closely behind—different breeds of the same race hunting together for each other's good. As they crest again, I sense an eye looking my way. I'm reassured mankind still has many lessons before reaching the wisdom of God's creatures.

The End

About the Author:

Robert Bergmann is a retired Marine living in the Tennessee Smokey Mountains.

To all who have sacrificed in the name of Peace, in the defense of Freedom, and in the justice for All.

Exit Wounds
by Lana Bella

In the summer of '93,
A war-heralded man I went to see
He told me of soldier's perils and veteran's pleas.

He perched on his armchair upon keen hinged thighs,
"My friends were slowly dying, yet I miraculously revived,
So 'Nam marched me home with bullets in my body and half a life."

From the stump of a man, the face wistfully frowned,
"While the world lived on, I became a scrap on solitary ground,
With visions of airborne shards and crimson wounds in ragged sounds.

No pat on the back, while paltry homage blessed by few,
The pockmarks of war, and stiff shells of terror my convivial crew,
Its soul gives life to wretched triumph, but then to whom was justice due?

Returning from a distant war, resuming those simple ways,
I grew frenzied as phantom corpses of battered grief merged gray
Yet who they were, I once had lain beside in those blood-rained days.

Like caged animals the war veterans were led in mortal blame,
I was not only psychologically scarred and physically maimed,

97

The nearby parishes with their contemptuous eyes also fixed me in shame.

So I passed into a man who no longer cared nor walked sure,
I drank in frantic jags, and so these mangled bones sped in haste at Death's door,
With downward sweeps it mattered not how I was wrought or insomnia-moored

But what was there to fear when salvation subsists?
For then appeared as a saving prayer a woman who to me enlists,
This lovely girl patched me whole and with dauntless words untwists.

Buzzing away like midnight flies on damp pillows' woes,
She nursed away my insomnia-fraught from fits of anguished throes,
I whom war'd discarded, given breath again as only unyielding kindness bestows.

Here I am, an amorous man in humbled cloth of working man-blue,
Taking leave proudly onto my land with amputated limbs and hollowed shoes,
But what I love most are the evenings where prettily strolls my darling Sue."

The End

About the Author:

Lana Bella has her work published with Deltona Howl, Thought Notebook, Earl of Plaid, Undertow Review and Global Poetry. She resides on some distant isle with her novelist husband and two frolicsome imps, where the sun shines, the birds chirp, and the sea foams in silvery waves.

To Warren Westdyke of the 82nd Airborne. I never met you, but you gave me the greatest gift anyone could ever ask for, a Mom who has always supported and encouraged me. For that, I will never stop thanking you.

Not Perfect, Still a Hero
by Jason W. Huschle

As a child I always believed, like most children, that my daddy could do no wrong. So strong and brave, he never cheated and he never told a lie. As a child, my daddy was perfect, and he was my hero.

It wasn't until I was on the verge of finishing high school that I realized just how naïve my beliefs had been.

At the time of my birth, my father had already been serving in the Marine Corps for two years. From what I've been told he planned on making it a career. Too young to remember much about his day-to-day life back then, I do remember the day that everything changed. Only five years old at the time, that day stands out as one of my earliest memories. Usually when he came home from work, he'd first play with me for a while as he asked my mother about her day. That day was different, though. I got barely a pat on the head as he took my mother into the kitchen. I never did hear what they said to each other, but when they came back into the living room I could see that my mother had been crying.

My father carried a large manila envelope. I would find out much later that it had contained his discharge orders. Not long after that day he stopped putting on a uniform every morning and started job hunting instead.

I never gave much thought to why my father left the military as I grew up. We moved away not long after his discharge was complete to take a new job he had been offered. He rarely ever spoke of his time served. In middle school they started teaching us about 9/11 and the immediate aftermath. I suppose I realized then that my father must have served during that timeframe, but he never mentioned it, and I never thought to question him.

Applying for college brought the full story to light. With no chance at getting enough money through standard financial aid alone to afford my degree, I began researching benefits available to the children of military veterans. Several options came up for children of service members who had served in Iraq or Afghanistan after the 9/11 attacks. I was so excited when I realized there was a chance I would be able to get my degree without having to take out any student loans.

With that excitement moving me, I ran up to my father as soon as he got home from work that day and told him how awesome it was that he had served after 9/11. He just stared at me in silence for a moment. Then, for the first time in my life, I witnessed my father break into tears. I didn't have a chance to apologize before he retreated to his bedroom upstairs. Several hours passed before I saw him again.

I tried asking my mother what had made him so upset, but she just claimed that it wasn't her place to tell me. She said I would have to talk to him myself when he felt ready to talk about it. She did give me one piece of advice, however.

"When he is ready to talk about it, you just listen. Don't talk. Listen."

When he finally came downstairs again my father had an armful of paperwork with him. He asked me to join him in the kitchen so we could talk about his time in the military. I found myself a little bit nervous. He still looked really shaken up, and I didn't want to upset him again. I thought about telling him we didn't have to, but he had already left the room. My mother gave me a gentle nudge, so I didn't have much choice but to follow.

He sat at the table with the stack of papers in front of him by the time I stepped into the kitchen. He pushed one of the stacks toward me as I sat down. At the top sat a military personnel file. I flipped it open and found myself looking at my father's discharge paperwork. My father had always kept himself physically fit, so I was shocked to see the words medical discharge in the subject line. My surprise must have been plain to see because he answered my question before I even had a chance to ask it.

"PTSD. It hit me hard after the deployment."

Post-traumatic stress disorder. I had heard the term before, mostly on the news. People with PTSD had trouble dealing with life after a war. It didn't make any sense to me, though. My father had a great job, and he always seemed happy at home. I rarely saw him and my mother fight about anything. PTSD just didn't seem possible for someone like him.

"I tried my best to just get on with my life when we got back from the first tour. Tried to stay focused on work and you and your mother. I was okay as long as I was busy. It was when things got quiet that I started having problems," he explained.

I stayed quiet when he stopped speaking. It seemed like he needed a moment to compose himself. Plus, I really had no idea what to say. It felt like I should say something comforting, but I honestly had no clue where to begin. How do you comfort someone when you weren't even really sure what was wrong with them? Instead, I started going through the rest of the paperwork in front of me.

Mostly medical bills and appointment slips, they dated all the way back to my father's time in the service. The most recent one, dated from just the month before, had come from a therapist at the local VA office. From what I could tell, he had been making visits at least once a month for a long time. In hindsight, I could recall several times when he'd gotten home late from work and not given a reason.

"Every once in a while when we were overseas, I would get assigned to a checkpoint detail," he finally continued. "It was pretty dull, mostly. Sometimes hours would go by without us seeing a single vehicle. When we did have one pass through it would be about five

101

minutes of work then back to sitting around again. Got to the point some days we almost wished something interesting would happen. It was a stupid thing to hope for, and then one day we got our wish."

He didn't seem on the verge of tears anymore. Instead, he looked off into the distance the way people do when they are remembering something important or emotional.

"There were four of us on detail when it happened. It was towards the end of our shift, and we were just waiting for our replacements to show up. A truck came rolling up to the checkpoint, so we all got into our usual positions, nothing different than what we had done a dozen times that day. It was my job to check the bed of the truck for anything suspicious. Whatever was in the back had a tarp over it, and that was always one of our big red flags."

His voice became a bit shakier now. Everything in me wanted to tell him to stop. I wanted to tell him it wasn't important, that he didn't have to tell me the rest. I followed my mother's advice, though, and stayed quiet.

"I gave a signal to the men at the front and waited while they adjusted their weapons. It wasn't much of a change. Most people wouldn't have noticed unless they knew what to look for. As it turned out, the driver knew exactly what to look for. I never saw what he did, but I heard one of the guys up front yell *bomb*. That's when everyone started firing. It was complete chaos. When everything calmed down, the driver was dead. We never did find out which one of us fired the kill shot. It could've easily been me.

"I'm not saying I wouldn't do it the same way again. We all did what had to be done at the time, and we were right to do it. There were enough explosives under that tarp to take down a building or two, and more than enough to kill the four of us. The driver had been reaching for the trigger. We probably weren't his actual target, but I think he panicked when he saw we were going to search the truck. Knowing it had to be done

102

didn't help me sleep any better at night. Even now there are some nights that I just can't sleep. I just stay awake for hours thinking about it."

He pointed to one of the appointment slips that I still had in my hand. I'd been so lost in his story that I hadn't realized I still held it.

"I tried going to therapy while I was still on active duty, but I just couldn't get my head straight. Just putting on the uniform every morning reminded me of what I had done. After a few months, the doctor made the call that I was no longer fit for duty. Some guys would have been angry about it, but even back then I knew he was making the right call. I couldn't keep myself focused on the job, and that's the kind of thing that can get people hurt or worse.

"The sessions I go to now help a lot more. Everyone there has been through something similar. It helps knowing I'm not the only one with problems. I've met a lot of men and women who had to do much worse."

He took a deep breath and did his best to give me a smile, but it didn't make his face look any less sad.

"I'm sorry I lost it when you brought up the war. I've gotten better, I really have, but even after all these years it still gets to me. I know I probably shouldn't have kept all this from you for so long, but it's still really hard to talk about. Tomorrow I'll help you with your application. I just can't do it tonight."

"You're getting help now, though," I finally said. "Eventually it won't bother you anymore, right?" I wanted so badly for that to be true, but I knew in my heart it wasn't.

"That's the problem, honey. It never goes away, not completely anyway. It never will either, and I'm not sure it would be a good thing if it did. What kind of person would I be if I could kill someone and not care about it?"

With that, he gathered up his paperwork and said goodnight. I stayed at the table for a while trying to take in everything I had just learned. I went to sleep that night still trying to process it all. In less than an hour, my father had become a much more complicated man then I had known throughout my entire childhood.

We didn't talk much about it over the next few days, except for the little bit of information I needed for my application. Still, the next time he attended a group therapy session I asked if I could go with him. I wanted to be a bigger part of helping him. He seemed a little hesitant, but he agreed to let me come.

My father was one of the first ones to speak that night. He told his story again. At the end, he introduced me to the group. It turns out that he had mentioned me before. He admitted that he hadn't told me sooner because he'd felt ashamed. He'd been afraid I would look at him differently if I had known.

It turns out he wasn't the only one with that fear. As the night went on, I listened to at least a dozen men and women share stories about the things they had been forced to do to survive and how their lives had been affected by it. Some of the stories were similar to what my father had shared with me, and some of them were much worse. Some of the speakers broke down and cried, unable to continue. There were others who didn't share their stories at all, but offered comforting words and advice to those who did.

The therapist gave me a turn to speak. I looked around the room wondering what I could possibly say that would make the slightest difference after all they had been through. Then it hit me. There was something I could offer them that even their therapist could not. I wrapped my arms around my father, and then looked back at all the men and women who had shared their troubles with me.

"I love my dad even more now that I know what he's been through. Your families will too. Don't be scared to tell them."

My relationship with my father changed dramatically the day he opened up to me. While his story may have shattered my childish illusions about his perfection, I will never regret having heard it. After eighteen years I finally met my real father, someone I had never even realized I'd missed. He isn't perfect by any definition of the word, and he certainly has his share of problems. Yet, now, he is even more of a hero to me than he'd ever been in the past.

I will never let him forget it.

The End

About the Author:

Born in May of 1983, Jason Huschle began writing at the age of fourteen. He joined the Marine Corps in 2007, where he served for five years. He spent time in both Iraq and Afghanistan, where he learned firsthand what deployments into a war zone can do to service members. Jason now lives in California where he spends his free time as a freelance writer.

Shadows of the Past
by SL Berg

Bill Carlin prepared to make his tent trip from the shores of Dover to Omaha Beach on the Normandy coast of France, to once again relive that horrible day of June 6, 1944. He always made sure to rent a small fishing boat two weeks in advance. He paid a premium price so that he would be the only passenger for the voyage. Bill had managed to rent the same boat *The Dover Queen* with Captain Huston at the helm as he had for the last eight years.

They cleared the dock and the shoreline at approximately five in the morning. Bill stood on deck in front of the wheel manned by Captain Huston. They moved out into open waters and through the interwoven grasses so prevalent in the spring. Slowly, the Queen moved further away from the shore and picked up speed. Bill stood perfectly still, his jacket zipped up to the neck. The wind always proved strongest in the area they moved through now. He knew that the wind would die down soon and the warmth of the sun would prevail. The moment he always waited for, that's when Bill would open his eyes wide and stare straight ahead.

Almost as if by a signal the winds died down and that trace of sunshine crossed his chin. Bill stared straight ahead, his eyes constantly moving from side to side looking for a distant shoreline. Actually, he knew that the shoreline would not be visible for another two hours, but he scanned the horizon like he always did. The further out the boat went, the warmer it got even as the wind continued to whip across his face as it always did in the early part of June. The time passed quickly until they were about a half hour off shore. Here, at this point in the trip, the transformation usually took place.

PFC Bill Carlin sat in the in the landing vessel right in front of the helmsman. His buddies sat on both sides and behind him. All the soldiers looked tense, determined, and almost solemn. They too stared straight ahead. The ride got pretty bumpy as the LST rode over and through the waves. Bill narrowed his eyes as the shoreline got closer. Three short blasts of a whistle alerted the troops to prepare to go ashore. They checked their weapons, ammunition and other equipment. A lot of prayers were being offered at that moment. Bill touched the upper left pocket of his fatigue jacket. The "Dear John" letter was there.

The ramp dropped, and the soldiers of Company A, 116th Regiment, of the 29th Infantry Division walked into the water. They raised their rifles above their heads to keep them dry. The water, shoulder high to most of the soldiers, caused some to panic. Unable to swim, some simply drowned as others passed by unable to help. Bullets and all sorts of hell hit all around them. Bill put his head down and started to make his way to the left where there were fewer explosions. As he began to feel the soft sand of the beach under his feet, he saw a soldier go down in a hail of fire from a German machine gun. Two other men stepped on a mine and died instantly from the explosion. Bill moved further to his left where he thought he could find some cover. He almost tripped over a body.

"Hey you, soldier, pick up the Browning and fire up to that machine gun nest on the hill to the left," an Officer, one of the few that was still alive, yelled orders to Bill and anyone else who could hear him.

Bill picked up the B.A.R and began to fire toward to the machine gun nest. That concentrated more fire on his position. He felt a burning sensation in his right shoulder and then a similar burning in his left thigh. He yelled for a medic. One quickly arrived. The Medic put a gauze bandage on the shoulder wound and covered it with tape. He looked at the thigh wound and simply put tape on it.

"That's just a flesh wound, but the shoulder might be a good one," the Medic stated.

Now Bill felt a little bit better about things, so he decided he had better get back to the war. He picked up

108

the B.A.R and began to fire up to where the machine gun was. At the same time he began crawling toward what looked like a path up the hill. As he moved up the incline, he kept stopping. He hoped not to attract the attention of the Germans who were firing the machine gun. When he got close enough, he ripped a hand grenade from his belt, pulled the pin, and counted to six. After that, he threw the grenade toward the machine gun. The grenade landed near where most of the firing came from. Putting his head down, he listened. *Rata tata rata. Boom.* The machine gun stopped firing. Bill crawled closer and looked up. He saw a German soldier with blood streaming down his face. He raced to his weapon and shot the soldier. The German fell to the ground with his eyes open, the look of death on his face. Bill lurched forward as he vomited and then fell into his own waste.

He picked his head up and shouted to himself, "Let's get the hell out of here."

He quickly moved through some brush. At that point, he heard some loud orders being barked in a language he assumed was German. He moved closer and saw six soldiers getting onto the truck. Bill crawled forward to outflank them; he was now almost behind them. He pulled out another grenade and lobbed it onto the bed of the truck. Hearing the explosion, the screams of those still alive and conscious hit his ears. Bill quickly shot those still alive and moved on.

After that, he decided to try to find his way back to the beach and his unit. He began to retrace his steps. Suddenly, he found himself on a narrow dirt road. He walked cautiously on the side of it, hoping to get closer to the American beachhead. A horse drawn wagon with an elderly man holding the reins came toward him on the other side of the road. The wagon stopped, and the man motioned for him to get in. He jumped on to the wagon and laid down with the B.A.R against his body ready to fire.

The farmer covered him with a piece of tarpaulin typically used to cover vegetables. Bill dozed off for a short while until awakened by voices speaking French. He held the B.A.R close to him ready to fire. He could feel somebody standing nearby. Suddenly, someone picked up the tarpaulin. A German soldier looked at him as if unsure of what to do. Bill shot him in the head and then shot the two others running to the wagon. The farmer frantically tried to leave the horrible scene. Bill covered himself as best he could as the wagon began to move.

He fell asleep again and awoke when the wagon stopped. The farmer helped him get out of the wagon and lead him to a barn where he could rest. He sat down on a bale of hay. The farmer left, closing the barn door behind him. When gunfire sounded again, he got up and peeked through a crack in the door. Soldiers moved toward the barn. He watched them as they came closer, recognizing them as British or Canadian troops that had probably landed nearby. He pushed the door open and walked out with his hands up. A jeep approached with an Officer and a driver.

The Officer identified himself as Major Ashley. They were with a Canadian airborne unit that had been part of the invasion force. Once Bill established his identity and unit, the Canadian medics began to treat him as best they could. Shortly thereafter, they transferred him back to the hospital ship. Once aboard, his wounds on his shoulder and thigh were immediately treated. On a more serious note, Bill showed symptoms of severe shock. So, he was seen by a Navy Psychiatrist and diagnosed with Post Traumatic Stress Syndrome. They then transferred him to a mental hospital near London being used by the military.

After refusing transfer to the USA for further care, he was granted asylum for the duration of the war. After the surrender of Germany, he again refused an offer for a transfer to a Veterans Administration Hospital. So, he spent the next twenty years in a civilian mental hospital in Leeds. The British Government paid for his care. After his discharge from the hospital he lived in Leeds was

110

employed by the public library.

His mind returning to the present, Bill waded into the water and began to walk toward Captain Houston's boat which approached him. When close enough, he jumped into the boat and immediately went below to change clothes. He changed back into the dry clothes he had boarded with to join Captain Huston for the trip back to Dover.

"Bill, I certainly appreciate the business, and I don't mind making the trip to Normandy with you, but I just can't understand why you want to make the same trip every June?"

"Captain, I really can't tell you why I keep going back. Sometimes I think that I will remember something that will allow me to close that chapter of my life. But, everything remains the same year after year. And, then I go back to my current life in Leeds where I have lived since 1945."

****

The following year Bill made several attempts to contact the Captain, but he continued to be unable to reach him. Finally, he received a notification that Captain Huston had passed several months ago. Some family members told Bill that they were planning to sell the boat. At first, he thought about finding another boat to help him make the trip into the past, but then he began to think about buying the Queen from the family. He could simply then hire the help he needed for the trip. When the sale became final, he renamed her *The Shores of Normandy*. So, he hired a Captain and a journeyman sailor to help him make the foray into the past.

They sailed from Dover on June 6th at five in the morning. As usual, the conditions were eerily like they were June 6, 1944. Cool, windy, and dark, clouds blocked the light from the moon and the stars. As they moved into the open waters of the channel, Bill began to tense up just as he always did at this stage of the voyage. The wind hit his eyes. So, he closed his eyelids

111

and momentarily enjoyed the stinging sensation, knowing full well that the warmth of sunlight would soon follow. After two hours of standing still, almost entranced, the wind stopped and the sun light took over. Bill began to scan the horizon for a glimpse of the Shores of Normandy.

He stared ahead into the empty space until he finally began to see the shadows of distant shores. Just like every trip, year after year, his whole body tensed up when he heard the whistle to prepare for landing. This threw him back in time again to 1945. Instinctively, he touched the upper left pocket of his fatigue jacket. The letter remained in there.

"I'll read it later and try to understand what the hell happened," he said out loud to himself.

They landed amid the chaos of war with machine gun fire, explosions, and death everywhere. Always the same, he covered the same ground and he saw the same soldiers. Germans, Americans, and their allies dead and wounded. He saw the agony of death on the faces of the mortally wounded, and he heard the screams of pain from the survivors. Only one thing changed in these flashbacks, he seemed to know what was going to happen. He anticipated each event. He felt as if he watched a movie that he did not a play part in. Before he knew it, it was over and he was on the hospital ship on his way back to England.

In reality, he stood on his boat. So again, he went below to change into his dry clothes. First, he reached into the pocket of his fatigue jacket where he had the infamous letter. He sat down to read it as he had so many times before.

May 30, 1944
Dear Bill,
Since you left I have been very lonely and unhappy. I miss your company, the fun we used to have together. The letters I get from you once a week just aren't enough for me. Chuck Moore has been coming around

112

*to keep me company and we like each other. He won't
be going into the Army. He has a job and he wants to
marry me. I am sure you will find someone else when
you come home.*
   Regards,
   Betsy

   Bill read the letter again and then three more times.
   "I think that I need to answer her letter," he muttered
to himself.
   When Bill got home to his little apartment, he threw
his things down and sat to answer Betsy's letter. He
finally knew what to write and how to explain what had
happened to him. Most importantly, he wanted to
reassure her that it would all work out for the both of
them.

   June 8, 1995
   Dear Betsy,
   *I received your letter just before I was sent into
combat. I read it many times but I could never figure out
what happened to us. I didn't know how to answer you. I
have been fighting the war for a very long time. I think I
finally understand that we have won. It's time to get back
to working on my future. I can come home. I will leave as
soon as I can. I hope to see you soon.*
   Love,
   Bill

   The next day Bill began to make plans to go home to
the USA. He booked passage on a freighter, wanting to
feel like he was arriving on a troop ship with all the other
soldiers. He packed some clothes, his discharge from
the US Army, his two purple hearts, silver star, and
infantry combat medal. Along with all of that, he included
the discharge papers from the mental hospital, plus
some pictures of him and his buddies just before they
went into combat. These things came in very handy as
he boarded the ship to go home. He had no passport or

113

other means of identification. They would also be necessary to pass through customs in the USA.

The trip across the Atlantic took nine days because of bad weather. They arrived in Baltimore June 30, 1995. He was delayed by customs as expected, and he had to repeat his story many times. When all was said and done, they welcomed a hero home. Given temporary documents, they allowed him to enter the country and apply for a passport. He exchanged his British currency for American dollars and bought a bus ticket to Topeka, Kansas where he and Betsy had formerly lived.

The taxi took him directly to 172 Oak Street. He got out of the taxi and told the driver to wait. The house looked abandoned, so he went next door and rang the bell. A woman came to the door.

"You don't look like a salesman, can I help you?" she said with a smile.

"Yes, I am looking for Mrs. Betsy Carlin. She used to live next door?" he stated, his throat constricted.

"The only Betsy I know that lived in that house was Betsy More. She moved after her husband passed away. Somebody told me that she had moved into one of those small apartments downtown. You know, mister, that was a long time ago. So let me ask, how did you know her?"

"It's a long story. We were married and the war separated us. Thanks for your help," he offered as politely as his anxiousness to find Betsy would allow.

He went downtown with the same cab and again told the driver to wait. Bill went into a three-story tenement house and inquired about Betsy More. By some miracle, someone remembered her.

"She moved into the retirement center about ten years ago," a very polite woman offered.

"Where is the center? I grew up here but I have been away a long time."

"It's off the State Route 219. You can't miss it."

"Thank you, I will head over there now," he offered as he moved to quickly leave.

Bill took the same cab to the Cedars Of Lebanon

Retirement Center. When he came in he felt sick. The place was run down and shabby at best. An odor of people who didn't bathe or shower regularly hung heavy in the air. He approached the front desk and asked for Betsy More.

"We have no guest named More at this time," the lady at the front desk stated.

"Actually, she may be using her maiden name again, that would be Betsy Sutton," he offered with haste.

"Yes, sir, Betsy Sutton is in room 213. Take the elevator at the end of the hall."

Bill stood in the doorway of room 213 and looked at the sleeping Betsy. She didn't look like the Betsy Sutton that he had married in 1942. Betsy opened her eyes and smiled.

"Hello, Bill. After Chuck got killed I'd hoped you would come back to me."

He walked over to her bedside, bent over, and kissed her on the forehead. Then, he smiled broadly.

"Bill, I haven't heard from you in such a long time. I assumed you had been killed," she said with an audible sigh.

"Well, you know I was in the Army, and I fought in the war. That was a long time ago. Then I fought my own war for many years. I can't tell you how many times I have gone back to France and landed in Normandy. I have been living in Leeds so that I could go to Normandy in early June just like the first time. I was wounded twice, but that didn't stop me the first time or every time after that. I only know that I have been very lonely since we said goodbye so long ago."

He looked at Betsy, but she was fast asleep. Bill folded his arms on the bed rail and he too fell asleep.

Bill woke up first and Betsy immediately after. They stared at each other. He saw a beautiful young woman, and she saw a handsome young man. They both liked what they saw.

"Betsy, we should get out of this place and find a place like where we lived before, where we can be together and live happily. You know I don't have to go back to France anymore. The war is finally over for me," he stated, hope elevating the tone of his voice.

"Bill, I'm so happy that your home," she sighed.

One hour later, they walked out of room 213 holding hands and smiling. They walked past the front desk as nurses, doctors, and patients cheered. From somewhere a familiar tune and words rang out.

It's still the same old story, a fight for love and glory, a case of do or die.

The world will always welcome lovers as time goes by.

Oh yes, the world will always welcome lovers as time goes by.

The End

About the Author:

SL Berg is a veteran as well as a 1960 graduate of NYU. An entrepreneur from 1960-1998, he founded a technology company that was taken public in 1989. Now a retired businessman residing in Sarasota, Florida, he enjoys writing. He's written two novels and many short stories. *Escape to Live* is his first published novel, which you can find on Amazon at:
http://www.amazon.com/Escape-Live-SL-Berg-ebook/dp/B003X4KWAS

*In loving memory of my father, Mort Morgan, whose pain
was overwhelmed by his love for his family.*

Finding 'Peace with Honor'
by Robert Morgan

Early in 1997, Kenneth "Mort" Morgan found himself
on a doctor's examination table preparing for a liver
biopsy. A few months earlier, at the suggestion of family
and friends, he had donated blood for the local VFW
blood drive. Weeks later, he received a letter saying he'd
tested positive for Hepatitis C. Now, nearly thirty years
since being wounded in Vietnam, where he likely
contracted the virus from a blood transfusion, Mort
reflected upon his past, the experiences and emotions of
his eventful life, and pondered what battles remained in
his future.

Proud Veteran for an Ungrateful Nation

"Vietnam…Ours was an ugly, dirty war from the day
the CIA stepped on its soil to the day Mr. Nixon gave us
'Peace with Honor' too many years and lives too late.
Our nation sent, and then spat, on the youths that fought
in this war that nobody either wanted or thought was
right. There was little home support for the 'troops over
there'. Few yellow ribbons were hung, no parades were
held. Just a ton of broken hearts, crushed dreams, and
lost youth." [1]

Mort Morgan had one goal as he started his senior
year of high school in 1966, to join the Army and serve in
Vietnam. Driven by the ideals of World War II veterans
like his father, the stirring words of President John F.
Kennedy, and the death of neighborhood friend Thomas
Vontor in Vietnam that year, the working class, suburban
Philadelphia native felt an unswerving duty to serve his
country in a time of war.

Ultimately, Staff Sergeant Morgan served two tours in
Vietnam as a member of the 1st Cavalry. Although
reluctant to listen to authority, he was still an able soldier

117

awarded the Bronze Star with Valor and three Purple Hearts during his service. In theatre from 1968 to 1970, he was involved in several major battles, including Operation Pershing, the Tet Offensive, Khe Sanh, and operations in Cambodia.

However, the country he joined the Army for in 1967 was not the same country he returned to after his first tour in 1969. Vietnam had left him disillusioned and confused. He understood peace protestors. He, himself, had sat outside the White House hoping for the chance to speak to President Nixon about withdrawing from Vietnam. What Mort could not understand was the misguided anger shown towards Vietnam Veterans themselves. What had they done besides served their country?

Unable to reconcile these feelings and facing military discipline for failing to obey lawful orders while on post stateside, Mort elected to return to Vietnam for a second tour. This time he returned lost, feeling abandoned, and suffering with what would be later called Post Traumatic Stress Disorder, or PTSD. With nowhere else to turn, Mort set out on the road to find his own "peace with honor" that President Nixon would announce years later at the end of the Vietnam War.

Stranger in a Strange Land

Even while lying back on the exam table, Mort couldn't stop the music in his head. Whether the Bob Dylan or Neil Young favorites he'd heard in the car ride this morning or the Leon Russell *Stranger in a Strange Land* tune he'd listened to last night, it seemed that Mort was always, poorly, carrying a tune.

Even though he couldn't read a line of music, the *Freedom Rock* soundtrack (as it was called in the late night TV ads in the 1980s) was part of his soul. "The artists of the time seemed to be inside your head, taking your thoughts and putting them to music." [2]

Their music also took him back to a different time and place.

118

"Upon returning from 'Nam…I kinda got lost. With what I just went through…and with what I saw in our nation, I was dumbfounded to say the very least. Nothing made sense: family, friends, co-workers, everything was different, and I didn't seem to fit in anymore, anywhere. The lessons and values learned as a child didn't fit in to this time either. Everyone and almost everything was a stranger. It took a long time to join the world again." [1]

After leaving Vietnam through most of the 1970s, Mort had bounced around finding odd jobs, which paid for room, board, alcohol, cigarettes, and drugs. His travels became legendary: watching a Volkswagen van roll off a cliff in Oregon, being arrested for *taking a shower* on the Vanderbilt University campus (a shower in the female dorm, that is), and living in a cabin in Mountain Pine, Arkansas.

These stories epitomized the animated and fun-loving side of Mort—the good part that everyone who met him knew and loved. They also hid the dark side of PTSD, heavy drug use, sleepless nights, and never fully accepting Vietnam.

Mort's travels would continue until, while in Tennessee, he met his future wife, Mary. As Mort would later write, "I'd have to say that Mary saved my life. Got me off the junk (heroin)…and was the first person who listened to me." In finding Mary, Mort found love and a confidant for life, no matter how much they disagreed. In finding Mort, Mary began healing a damaged soul. Together, they created a family that would become the cornerstone of Mort's return to the world.

Family First

How am I going to tell them the news? Mort thought after discussing the results of the biopsy with his doctor. A diagnosis of advanced Hepatitis C had been confirmed with limited treatment options available. More depressingly, Mort was given a lifespan of *about five years or so*. This would be the first of three different *about five years or so* discussions he would have with the doctor.

Mort wanted none of it. *I've been shot, stabbed and blown up and jumped up and got back into the jungle,* he thought to himself. *And now I have to deal with this!*

As Mort pondered what this diagnosis would mean to his wife and children, he thought about what they had meant to him. As many have described, returning to life after war is difficult. For Vietnam veterans, the return to American society was particularly challenging because of the fervent opposition to the war and those who served in it. Mort's return had been no different, but with love and family, he pieced his life back together.

For Mort, reconciliation was more than just building a family. It was building a *loving* family that cared for each other and maintained relationships with parents and siblings Mort felt that family meant taking an active part his children's lives, saying *sorry* when his work with veterans overran into family events, and locking up the demons of his past. *Family first* was more than just his motto—it was the golden his rule for the Morgan house.

Mort actually never stopped believing in *family first*, even in Vietnam. He was proud to be a Morgan. He fondly told the story of how, in Vietnam, he grabbed the shoulder of General Westmoreland to try and catch a helicopter ride to another part of Vietnam where one of his brothers was stationed. He talked proudly about seeing another of his brothers play one college football game for the University of Michigan, or hearing just how good his younger brother was playing in high school football. Mort never gave up on his family; he just stopped going to them when he needed it.

Mort's manifestation of PTSD was that he believed no one could help him. He felt destined to suffer alone. Even his beloved Mary, who he could talk to, could not understand what he saw and how it felt. It was not until years later when his father, the decorated World War II veteran, had begun telling his war stories that Mort realized that his parents and siblings could have helped him in dealing with Vietnam. Just like how he had taught his children to be there for one another in times of distress.

Now, with a diagnosis of an incurable virus with limited treatment options available in 1997, he was going to need them for support like never before. More importantly to him, with three children still yet to graduate high school, they needed him just as much.

Honor and Duty

As Mort leaned back in his chair, he stared across the large round table full of beer, cigarettes, and relaxed uniform covers, to a spot on the far side wall. Fixated on nothing in particular, Mort sat there physically and emotionally drained after another long weekend honoring fallen veterans for Memorial Day. Just a few months after being diagnosed with Hepatitis C, Mort already felt the side effects of the new medicine: nausea, dizziness, and chronic fatigue. He wondered how much more he could take.

For Mort, serving as a member of the local VFW Memorial Team, marching in parades and performing military funeral services became his duty to his country and to the veterans who did not come home. He felt a near unparalleled need for remembrance of his fallen brothers in arms, ensuring that their sacrifice would not be forgotten. Mort would sacrifice time spent with his own children to ensure that Memorial Team business was properly attended to.

Mort glanced down at his arms, feeling and rubbing the metal band around his left wrist. Inscribed on the metal band was *John C. Hill*. This *KIA* (Killed in Action) bracelet served as a constant reminder for Mort of why he soldiered on with the Memorial Day weekend services, despite his own health condition.

John C. Hill had been Mort's best friend in Vietnam. Meeting in boot camp from nearby Irvington, New Jersey, John and Mort served together nearly every day until John's untimely death at the hands of a *teenage girl* (as Mort would describe) with an AK47. Serving on the Memorial Team, Mort honored John and the others who died in Vietnam and other wars.

Memorial Team service offered Mort an outlet for the trauma of the Vietnam War. It provided him some honorable sense of closure, though never forgetting. No matter how he felt, he knew he could not let those guys like John C. Hill down. Nor would he let them down.

Death on the Home Front

In the years after his initial Hepatitis C diagnosis, Mort's physical health continued to deteriorate from the side effects of medication. Mort also suffered from an emotional roller coaster fueled by depression and PTSD. At times, the search for *peace with honor* was replaced by the goal of daily survival.

Yet, in 2003, Mort would be called to duty like no time before. The town that Mort had called home for fifteen years had lost one of its own to the Iraq War. Corey Small, a schoolmate to his kids and relative of a family friend, had become the first person since World War II to die in combat from this community.

Mort became a spokesperson for the family, dealing with media requests as they recovered from the tragedy. Their nightmare would only worsen later in the year as reports surfaced that their son had committed suicide shortly after speaking to his wife and newborn child. A wave of questions arose: How could he? Why? Was he a coward? Mort had to draw on his own experiences to provide some answers.

"A lot of people can't understand how a man in a war would take his own life," Mort was quoted as saying. [3] He understood just how difficult it is for a soldier, missing his family and friends, and missing life before *seeing your first dead body*. Mort knew how grim the world could look, and how appealing death could be. He had witnessed it himself in Vietnam.

The young soldier's tragedy only intensified Mort's own personal battles. Unable to work due to his

122

illnesses, he tried to channel his energies into serving veterans and honoring fallen soldiers. However, his physical health, the years of Hepatitis C treatment, prevented him from doing more, causing him to slip into a darker depressive state. More sleepless nights, more bitterness, and less hope prevailed.

Peace and the Future

About ten years later, Mort sat on a porch on a beautiful late summer day. A school bus pulled up and dropped off a young child after his first day of kindergarten. The child, a slightly blonder version of another of Mort's sons, refused to talk to anyone except his *Daddio*. Only Daddio could understand the day he'd had.

For Mort, he was seeing his legacy unfold. Here was his oldest grandson, coming home from his first day of school. His grandson had quite a day–he already had two girlfriends! Of course, Daddio knew something about that, as he once had two girlfriends as well (in high school though!).

All and all, Mort had found happiness. Over the years, he continued to visit his siblings, particularly his sister's family on holidays. He had walked one of his daughters down the aisle in the same outfit he wore some thirty years earlier for his own wedding. He had seen his children grow up into respectable adults. He now had four grandchildren to torture his children with.

He never stopped serving veterans. Unbeknownst to his family, he ran a support group online for veterans suffering from PTSD. Mort discussed his personal demons with other veterans to aid them in their own battles. He began building a journal of his time in Vietnam, describing the people he had met and places he had served along with information about what it was really like. Mort, never a rich person, made routine donations each month to various veterans' charities, such as the Wounded Warrior Project and Disabled American Veterans.

Ultimately, Mort continued honoring the brothers who never came home by supporting those who did. While he always kept his fallen brothers like John C. Hill in his heart, he had finally been able to bury them.

A few weeks after seeing his grandson come home from his first day of school, Mort would be treated by his children to see his beloved Philadelphia Eagles. It was a wonderful, but bittersweet time, as Mort was unable to walk much. The years of damage caused by cigarettes, Hepatitis C treatments, and other various ailments had sapped the life out of him.

Shortly after this football game, Mort's health worsened beyond the point of recovery. He passed away after sixty-five years of living life on his own terms.

Peace with Honor

While President Nixon spoke of ending the Vietnam War with *peace with honor*, the scars inflicted on the psyche of soldiers like Mort took years, if ever, to fully heal. For Vietnam veterans like Mort, it took years, if ever, to find peace. Mort's *peace* came from his love and devotion to family and watching his children grow up.

As for *honor*, well, only when American society realized their mistakes in its treatment of Vietnam veterans some twenty-five years later were they *honored* for their service. However, Mort found his own *honor* through his service supporting veterans, both living and passed. He found peace with the horrors he was a part of in Vietnam. He helped ease many a family's pain by performing military honors or just talking to them. He shared his experiences and emotions with a younger generation of soldiers to help them deal with PTSD.

It may have taken over forty years, but President Nixon was right. Mort Morgan was able to end the Vietnam War with *peace with honor*. Not by leaving the service, or seeing the war end, but through a lifetime of service to family and veterans.

Bibliography:
Paraphrased with permission from:
(1) http://blackknights4.tripod.com/index.html
(2) http://blackknights4.tripod.com/id11.html
Direct quote from:
(3)
http://usatoday30.usatoday.com/news/nation/2003-10-12-suicide-inside-usat_x.htm

About the Author:

Robert Morgan is a freelance writer originally from East Berlin, PA, now residing in New England. A U.S. Navy veteran, he served onboard the USS Dallas and at the Submarine Support Unit in Groton, CT. RI Bert is also an engineer, earning a Bachelor's degree in Nuclear Engineering Technologies from Thomas Edison State College in Newark, NJ.

A Soldier's Cry
by Kelley Hutchison

Dredge deep
within the trenches
the shame, the guilt, the debris
mercy have no meaning
from harm's wrath and misery
fatigue, a foe of darkness
where reality lacks allure
incognizance blurs the vision
of freedom's open door
pure thought, allegiance
empty in their wells
poisoned by a venom,
circumstances and hell
strike those
that lack indifference
not annihilate the free
take count the hours given
for love of liberties
a soldier born to glory,
a rationale and true belief
conscientious is the victor
sacrificial to release

About the Author:

A creative writer, poet and educator, residing in
Southern California, Ms. Hutchison's work encompasses
contributions to various websites, blogs and biographies.
She has a well received selection of personal poetry in
print and another in the works. Writing is her first
passion.

She is a New England native and frequent visitor to the
area, where her writing flourishes with the changing
landscape.

This story is dedicated to my father, William David Quinn, who served in Vietnam 1966-1967, as well as all who have sacrificed so much to serve our country.

I wrote this fictional story laced with tidbits of truths from several sources for varied reasons, the most basic of which is to say, in my own small way, "Welcome Home, Daddy" to my father, who after all he sacrificed in Vietnam didn't come home to the hero's welcome he deserved. As long as I breathe, I will never get over that.

Coming Back To Life
by Kiki Howell

As the images from the memory he shared solidified in my brain, a plague of guilt grew in accordance with my desire to erase them.

"We were told to find something to send home for the family to bury," my father's voice cracked.

I squirmed, as much an attempt to alleviate the ache in my back from having sat for hours now in waiting room chairs at the hospital, as it was an unconscious desire to leave the room. In the vein of giving heed to common turns of phrase, the words, "be careful what you wish for," rang through my thoughts, and hung heavy with the weight of their truth.

What I'd hoped for, aspired to really, was to have my father open up to me. To have him really talk to me, to be given the chance to help him overcome the war he repressed, had begun to come to pass. Rather than elated, I sat here shell-shocked for lack of a better term. My heart beat wildly in my chest. I trembled as my eyes scanned my surroundings.

"There on the ground was a piece…small…"

He'd tripped over several words, swallowed hard between them, so that I could barely make them out. Several syllables slurred together, but I wasn't about to ask him to repeat himself. Even with my degree in military social work, I suddenly found myself not up for

129

the task. Here, in this moment, I repressed back to a girl, sitting in the living room, hidden but peering around the corner into the shadows of the dining room where my father sat on the floor hugging his legs, crying, after hearing the air raid sirens on the news.

I forced my eyes to the painting of a flower, slapped together with broad strokes of a metallic, blood red, which hung on the wall across from me. He wouldn't notice my attempt at a moment's distraction as he studied the faded and stained blue carpet on the floor. Our dining room had had blue carpet, though plush and a more royal color. I shook off the wayward thought as his voice came muffled by an attempt to hold back tears.

"With his red hair…curly…like…"

Our eyes met. His remained glassy and reddish from the exhaustion of the day, although now so much more so that they looked painful. Swallowing so hard again that I could hear it, my father shook his head. Here, in this public waiting room, his hands shook as he lost the battle to find a place to hide them. Defeated, he gripped the arms of the chair. His back didn't rest against the cushion any longer, and his legs seemed poised to get up and run.

With a strange dawn of recognition showing, my body mimicked his and braced to not overreact to the shiver that crawled over my spine like icy fingers tapping out a horror movie-themed tune. I forced a faked relaxation, muscle by muscle down my body, as my eyes fell back to the painting. The semi-impressionistic leaves resembled broad swords at first, but then dissolved into blades of grass in the Vietnam jungle I'd seen in movies. Frowning at the symbolism, I sighed, followed my rule to never analyze myself, not even for a second.

"I don't know why this memory just came to me…" he huffed, the sound dull and deep, raspy from the dehydration born of overindulgence in coffee and emotional exhaustion. "It came out of nowhere. I've not thought about that incident in almost forty years, like it didn't exist in my brain, like it never happened, and

130

today, here…" His voice had lost a little volume with each word he tried to force out.

Worn out, stress lined his aging face more predominately than it had just hours ago. His distant look alerted me that part of his mind remained in another time and place, one different in all ways, but as horrible to him as this moment sitting waiting for news of his severely injured son.

"The memory…it came to me like it happened yesterday. Vivid like those damn dreams."

"You're stressed…worried about James," I stumbled for something to say.

I mean, what could I say? Training or not, there were no words, at least none I'd been given that were appropriate enough, meant enough, conveyed enough, when someone shared that they'd looked for parts of a human in a war zone, no matter how small, just to send something home for the family to bury. Our language failed the human heart in that respect. Even lending a compassionate ear, while going a long way toward healing, fell short in my book. What could I give him, give any of them, for what ailed them, to make them something close to whole again?

Unfortunately, I'd heard similar stories too numerous to count before at work. Many years ago a janitor where I worked, a Vietnam Veteran like my dad, had said that vets should only talk to vets. One reason, for him personally, he'd said, was that he didn't feel he could burden his family with his memories, the horror of them. He wanted to protect their luxury of not knowing what he'd done within the atrocities of war. An honorable hero to the end like so many of them, no matter how high the personal price they paid daily, hourly, and for some minute by minute.

Maybe he'd been on to something there. Yet, most of my life I'd asked my dad questions about the war. Looking back, once in eighth grade I'd done my history project on the Vietnam War. I remember being a little disappointed in what little information I'd gotten from my

131

father at the time. Now, as I sat here, stunned, shocked, sick, I felt regret for having ever bothered him on the subject.

I didn't need my degree to figure out why I'd chosen the profession I had. For years, unable to get my father to talk, to come to life, to fix him, maybe selfishly so he'd be my dad fully, I'd made it my mission to help those like him by helping veterans deal with not only memories of the war they'd fought but to live the life they had now. Many times I'd witnessed patients of mine go from a shaking rage to trembling tears in seconds, to go through a whole range of emotions in the short amount of time they were with me. Yet, now that my father had finally opened up to some small degree, none of my book smarts, none of my empathy, none of my desperate drive to help kicked in. Instead, I resembled more a deer in headlights.

I'd been worried beyond description for hours now as well, about my half-brother laying somewhere, just a few walls away, on an operating room table as doctors tried to save his life, one they'd not given us much hope for. He'd been in a car accident, hit a telephone pole and been thrown through the windshield. My father had gotten the call parents dread at about two in the morning. So here we sat, knowing the sun had just begun to rise though we couldn't see it in our windowless room, waiting for news. Just when you don't think you can take another thing, another comes. It made sense according to the textbooks. One tragedy sets off repressed memories of another trauma.

My textbooks had given me glimpses of my dad along with shreds of peace granted by understanding. At least the books had explained to me to some degree why he'd always been so distant, so emotionally unavailable, so quiet and withdrawn. In fact, he'd been too textbook. Issues of life before the war obviously dictated the way a soldier dealt with the war.

Don't get me wrong, he tried very hard to be the best father he could. He showed up at all the big events in my life, he even said the right words, but part of him just wasn't there. There was a part of him he didn't have to give because he'd numbed himself to life to be able to numb himself to the war. Yes, that was my diagnosis. For my father, a distant mother coupled with the anger he faced coming back to the States after the war didn't help at all with his dealing with the atrocities he faced in that distant land. Didn't take a genius to put that theory together, but I wished that one would come up with a way to pick up the pieces in the aftermath.

"James' surgery has to be almost over," I changed the subject.

I felt so riddled with guilt, a failure for having nothing wise to say to him now that he'd shared. Not the first time I'd condemned myself in this sort of situation. A perfectionist should never be a social worker. I'd set myself up for a life of failure, fighting for my patients often when they refused to fight for themselves, fighting the system when at times red tape fought against its original goals, and so on. As usual, I comforted myself with the notion that sometimes all someone needed was a good listener. Maybe just a crap line, but right now, I grabbed onto it hook, line and sinker.

I looked over at James' mother. She sat alone, slumped over an open magazine though her eyes were obviously engrossed in the ever interesting carpet. Although pretty much a stranger to me, I'd tried to comfort her earlier after the doctor had informed us of the emergency surgery that needed to be done if they could just stabilize him.

"He has to live," my father grunted in an urgent whisper. Unsure who he'd spoken to exactly, still I nodded.

He placed his had gingerly, for just the briefest second, on mine. I could still feel them shaking, clammy.

"Sorry. I don't know what I'm saying…what I'm doing. Never in my life have I felt so scared, so angry, so guilty. It makes no sense," he rambled on.

133

The string of feeling words from a man who'd often appeared dead to the world left me unsettled to deal with my own trembling, my heart throbbing in my chest, as I prayed not to hyperventilate and pass out. No one needed that added incident.

"Don't apologize. There's no right or wrong way to act or feel in such a moment." That was textbook, but I'd nothing better, so I rambled on. "Not sure I have anything helpful to say, but I can listen."

There, some guilt alleviated, I guessed, or at least it should've been. I didn't buy what I was selling. He nodded.

"It's so quiet here I can't stand it. You know, no one prepares you for the noise of a war zone, for the injuries that become your loudest nightmares."

"It's okay," I whispered, hoping through juxtaposition to show him how loud he spoke. Although we were the only ones in the room, and James' mother hadn't flinched.

After all these years of silence, his invisible wounds took verbal form. I'd read once, who knows where, a veteran say that all men die in war. I knew that to be true of my father. His brothers and sisters had confirmed that he had not returned the same man he'd been before. I wanted to know the man he'd left as in October of 1966. I felt I'd been cheated of him. My dad's sister referred to him as a class clown in grade school, and the life of the party in high school. *Really? My dad?* Not that I didn't love my father, wasn't grateful for every moment of his time he'd so selflessly given me, but I wanted to meet that guy, the man he could have become. Just curiosity really rooted in an unfathomable truth.

Speaking of unfathomable truth, how many times as a young teen had I snuck to watch war movies when I stayed at my mom's house? I'd long lost count. As frequently as I had snuck to go through the box in the top of his closet when I'd stayed with him but he wasn't home. I'd finger his camera, the one with the piece of shrapnel still in it that had been in his pocket the day

134

he'd been injured in Vietnam. The violent way the black metal by the lens, silver on the ends now, poised inward, creating a hole would make my stomach clench at the brief thought of the same type of ammunition ripping into my father's flesh as it had that camera.

His medals, a Purple Heart and Bronze Star, left me in awe that these items meant so little to him that he never took them out. I'd discovered them on accident. My mother had told me when I'd questioned her about dad's box that he'd shoved it in a closet when they were together and had told her not to ask.

For me though, the words in the yellowed, folded into a square, letter that had accompanied the medals I practically had memorized. The phrase, *for heroism while engaged,* brought an awe of hero worship to my mind, something I could never relay to him even if I'd been allowed to speak the words, because words would fail to describe it. *Under intense enemy fire he exited the aircraft* amped that awe up another notch with trying to imagine fear I'd never comprehend. *Against a hostile force, heavy enemy automatic weapons, assisting the medical evacuation of the critically wounded, was instrumental, darkness closing in, and fragments tearing into his body*, all left me dizzy in an unexplainable vortex of sympathy and pride. It remained my luxury to not understand these statements from experience, to stop a war movie when it became too much, and to close a book about war to wipe my own tears.

Maybe someday I'd be able to tell him that I'd memorized the final line. *Although seriously wounded his outstanding display of aggressiveness, devotion to duty, and personal bravery is in keeping with the highest standards of the military service and reflects great credit upon himself, his unit, and the United States Army.* An avid book reader, I never had a line read so wondrously, conjured such emotion deep inside my soul so that I could barely breathe for dealing with them. Would he never know the amazing man I thought he was?

A doctor clad from head to toe in blue flew through the door, interrupting my reflections. I clamped down my lips over a startled shriek. He stopped short between us. "The surgery is over and he's stable."

My father hugged me, his body wracked with sobs. I went back to that glimpse I'd had of him crying once before, years ago when I'd found him in that dark room after hearing the air raid sirens on TV during the beginning of Desert Storm. I hadn't been able to hug him then, but I could now. Any emotion proved a start. My half-brother would live, and maybe, just maybe, my father could come back to life.

The End

About the Author:

Kiki Howell graduated from Kent State University with a Secondary English Education degree in 1993. She's been a published author since 2007, currently having over fifty stories published with several different small presses.

She's worked as a publishing administrator and an editor, and has successfully self-published a few of her own stories over the last few years.

Kiki was an Ohioana Author in 2011 and her most recent paranormal romance novels, *Hidden Salem* and *What Lies Within Us*, have hit several Top 100 Category Bestsellers Lists on Amazon.

Visit www.kikihowell.com for more information.

For my Dad, thanks for always being a shining example of a man!

My Dad, My Hero
by Stephen Quinn

I was the boy who loved army toys and spent days playing war with my friends.
We marched through the hills while dad worked and paid bills. But at night, sometimes he'd tell us tales.
My heart would race when I'd see dad's face, in photographs from a place called Vietnam.
He was a soldier ya see and hero to me. He fought to keep our country strong.
I'd watch him mow the lawn and wonder where he'd gone and the brave things he must have done.
But little did I know he'd had to go. He saw things that would tear him up inside.
That doesn't seem right, Dad was forced to fight. And his wounds are healing still today.
And what about all the men that died and the moms that cried. What reason could there be for so much pain?
Now I'm no longer a boy, no need for army toys. And War is certainly not something I wanna play.
Although my views on war changed, there is one thing that remains…My Dad, he's still a hero to me!

About the Author:

Stephen Quinn is a TV producer, Writer and sometime Artist. His Fathers experience with the Vietnam War and life there after has had a major impact on his life.

Even though, *We Go On*

Service *So Others May Live* betrays, and
Service Before Self caused wounds that fester still
Duty First, continues though current roles prove difficult
Not Self, but Country continues as spouse, parent, friend

And, *We Go On*

All values of *Selfless-Service* fall victim to irony
Being All You Can Be fails miserably
No Sacrifices Too Great holds an unbearable weight
Having fallen to the distorted value of *Integrity*

Regardless, *We Go On*

Proof

Made in the USA
Charleston, SC
13 February 2015